"You know, Mack, I'd have made you as a player. What's the matter? Got some kind of lawyer rule against kissing a client?"

He swallowed, unsure how to answer her. The thing was, he *was* a player—when the game was being played by his rules, which this game was not.

He allowed himself a small smile at her brazen challenge.

Watch out, Miss Martin, he said to himself. *This game's about to change.*

"Well?" she taunted.

"You don't know what you're doing," he said softly, the smile still in place.

"What do you mean?" she asked, feigning innocence.

"Oh, it's not your fault. You've only had boys to play with. It's understandable that you don't know what you're getting into by flirting with a man. I'd advise you to stop now."

"Stop?" she said as a flush rose all the way to her cheeks. "I don't want to stop."

SANCTUARY IN CHEF VOLEUR

—

MALLORY KANE

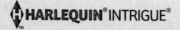

Recycling programs
for this product may
not exist in your area.

For Anna, who has been so supportive.
Thanks for understanding how it can be.

ISBN-13: 978-0-373-69775-5

SANCTUARY IN CHEF VOLEUR

Copyright © 2014 by Rickey R. Mallory

Printed in U.S.A.

ABOUT THE AUTHOR

Mallory Kane has two very good reasons for loving reading and writing. Her mother was a librarian, and taught her to love and respect books as a precious resource. Her father could hold listeners spellbound for hours with his stories. He was always her biggest fan.

She loves romantic suspense with dangerous heroes and dauntless heroines, and enjoys tossing in a bit of her medical knowledge for an extra dose of intrigue. After twenty-five books published, Mallory is still amazed and thrilled that she actually gets to make up stories for a living.

Mallory lives in Tennessee with her computer-genius husband and three exceptionally intelligent cats. She enjoys hearing from readers. You can write her at mallory@mallorykane.com or via Harlequin Books.

Books by Mallory Kane

HARLEQUIN INTRIGUE

CAST OF CHARACTERS

Hannah Martin—When Hannah witnesses the murder of her mother's boyfriend, she runs for her life, ending up in New Orleans, where she meets private investigator Mack Griffin.

MacEllis "Mack" Griffin—Mack decides to investigate Hannah while helping her find her kidnapped mother. Despite the danger he faces to protect her, his biggest fear is falling for the stubborn young blonde who has already half captured his heart.

Billy Joe Campbell—Hannah witnesses Billy Joe's murder by a drug lord's henchman, and now she's next on his list.

Hoyt—Hoyt is a hit man who knows which side of his bread is buttered. His job is enforcement, and he's good at it. But as he chases Hannah and Mack, he's unwittingly carving a path that will change the lives of everyone involved.

Chapter One

Hannah Martin's heart leaped into her throat as she waved at Mr. Jones, their neighbor, whose house was a mile away from theirs. He was watering his window boxes as she drove past.

Billy Joe had told her to be friendly with the neighbors but not to talk to them. "If you say one word to anyone, you'll never see Stephanie alive," he'd told her more than a few times in the past twenty-four hours.

Her mom, Stephanie Clemens, had gone into liver failure from cirrhosis a couple of weeks ago and was receiving hemodialysis while waiting for a donor liver. Then two days ago, Hannah had overheard Billy Joe, her mother's boyfriend, talking on his cell phone. He was arranging some kind of delivery to Tulsa, Oklahoma. And from his side of the conversation, it was obvious to Hannah that the goods were illegal and very valuable. It had to be drugs.

She'd confronted him and kicked him out of her mother's house, saying if he showed back up, she'd go to the sheriff. He'd left.

Then, yesterday, when she'd returned from a short run to the drugstore, her mother was gone and Billy Joe was back. He'd abducted her mom and was holding her somewhere.

Hannah growled in frustration and desperation as she pulled into the driveway of her mother's house. Popping the trunk lid, she grabbed one heavy case of beer, leaving the other case for a second trip.

"Billy Joe?" she called as she hooked her index finger around the handle of the screen door and then toed it open enough to catch it with her elbow. "Billy Joe? I'm back. My car's battery died again. That's why I took the Toyota."

She set the beer on the kitchen counter and listened. Nothing. The house felt empty. Where was he? He was always waiting at the door to make sure she got back from the grocery store not one minute later than he'd told her to be—with his cigarettes and beer.

An ominous thought occurred to her. Had something happened to her mother? She went through the house, but as she'd known, it was empty. Billy Joe wasn't there. Nearly panicked, she ran back outside. The setting sun reflected on the tin roof of the garage, but she thought she could see a light on inside it. Billy Joe never left a room without turning off the light, just like he never left the house without checking the locks three times. And woe to anyone who didn't put a tool or a book or even a ballpoint pen back exactly where they got it, down to the millimeter. So if the lights were on in the garage, then Billy Joe was in there.

From the first moment her mother had let him move in a few months ago, he'd taken over the garage. He'd kept it locked and never let her or Hannah near it. His reasoning was because he was working on his prized vintage Mustang Cobra and the engine had to stay free of dust. He was as obsessive about his cars as everything else.

Hannah walked across the driveway to the garage,

her shoulders stiff, her heart thudding so hard it physically hurt. Maybe her mother was in there? It wasn't the first time she'd thought that, but she was genuinely afraid of Billy Joe. After all, he'd pushed and slapped her mother a couple of times.

She wasn't sure what she thought—or hoped—to find when she looked through the glass panes of the side door, but she couldn't continue to sit by and do nothing while her mother was missing. Luckily, she'd just had her dialysis and wouldn't need it again until the end of the week. But Hannah didn't trust Billy Joe to take care of her. So although her stomach was already churning with nausea and a painful headache was making her light-headed, she was determined to see the inside of the garage.

Then she heard Billy Joe's voice. She nearly jumped out of her skin. In the first instant, she thought he was yelling at her. But by the time she'd heard three or four unintelligible words, she realized that his tone wasn't angry, it was afraid. Then she heard another voice. It was low and menacing, and she didn't recognize it.

With horrible visions swirling in her head of her mother dying while Billy Joe and some buddy of his drank beer, she approached the door cautiously. She slid sideways along the outside wall until she was close enough to see through the glass panes, her heart beating so loudly in her ears that she was positive the people inside could hear it.

When she peeked through the dusty glass panes, Billy Joe's back was to her, so she couldn't see his face. He was standing in front of his workbench, arms spread plaintively, talking in an oddly meek voice.

Her gaze slid to the man standing in front of him. He was twice the size of Billy Joe. Not quite as tall but *much* larger. He had on a dark, dull-colored T-shirt that fit his weightlifter's torso and beefy biceps like a glove. On the back of his right wrist was a tattoo. It was red and heart-shaped with what looked like letters in the center. Hannah blinked and squinted. Did it say MOM? She thought so, although the *O* wasn't exactly an *O*. It was a dark circle. Before she could focus on it, the man reached behind his back and pulled a gun. The fluorescent light glinted off the steel barrel. Hannah stared at it, her pulse hammering in her throat.

Billy Joe froze in place. His voice took on an edge of shrill panic and he stepped backward and turned his palms out. "Hey, man, watch out with that thing. It could go off." He laughed nervously. "I swear! You know everything I know. I'd never cheat the boss. I ain't that stupid."

Hannah saw a quick smirk flash across the other man's face and knew he was thinking the same thing she was. Billy Joe *was* pretty stupid.

"So what happened to the drugs and the money?" the man said, not raising his voice. "Because our customer says he was shorted, and the last payment you sent to Mr. Ficone was short, as well. Mr. Ficone depends on his distributors to pay him so he can pay his suppliers. Now his suppliers are expecting to be paid everything they're owed when Mr. Ficone meets with them in three days. So you've got three days to get that money to him."

"I don't know what happened to them, man. I had to use a new courier because my regular guy got picked up for not paying child support. Maybe he took it. I swear it was all there when I sealed the envelope. Or, hey, it coulda been the girl. Hannah Martin. My girlfriend's daughter. Smart-mouthed bitch." Billy Joe was sweating, literally. "She's always snooping around. She probably stole the money out of the envelope. That new guy coulda left it lying around."

The man with the red tattoo looked bored and disgusted. "I don't think Mr. Ficone's going to be satisfied with *somebody else must have done it.* He doesn't like people that can't control their people. That delivery was short almost twenty grand."

"Twenty? That's im-impossible," Billy Joe stammered.

Beneath the fear, Hannah heard something in his voice she'd heard before. Billy Joe was lying.

He took another step backward, toward the door. "I'm telling you, it had to be Hannah Martin. She's as sneaky as a fox. She musta got into it. I wouldn't be surprised. But I swear, when I sealed that envelope, it was all there. I counted it."

Hannah felt a heavy dread settle onto her chest, making it hard for her to breathe. He was throwing her to the wolves. She'd known he was trouble the minute she'd first laid eyes on him, and she'd tried to tell her mother, but Stephanie had never been smart when it came to men.

The man with the red tattoo shook his head. "Money doesn't disappear from a sealed envelope," he said. "I've got better things to do than stand here and listen to you lie. Mr. Ficone needs his money and he needs the drugs that were missing from your last delivery to our customer in Tulsa."

"But, man, I swear—"

"Shut up with your whining," the man yelled. "Where's the money?"

Hannah jumped at the man's suddenly raised voice.

She shrank back against the wall by the door, terrified. He was holding a very big gun and his voice told her he was sick of Billy Joe's rambling excuses.

What if he shot him? Everything inside her screamed "no!" Billy Joe was the only person in the world who knew where her mother was. She wanted to burst into the garage and beg the man to make Billy Joe tell her where her mother was, but the man looked ruthless and he was already sick of Billy Joe's whining. If she called attention to herself, he was liable to shoot her, too.

"All right, punk. Mr. Ficone has no use for you if you're not going to talk about where the money and the drugs are. That's all he wants."

Hannah shifted until she could see through the door again. She saw the man lift the barrel of the gun slightly, aiming it at Billy Joe.

"What he doesn't want is screwups like you working for him. He hates people who can't control their women. He hates thieves and he sure as hell hates loose ends."

"Listen. I'll get the money back. I've got a plan," Billy Joe said, his hands doubling into fists. "My girl-friend's sick. Real sick. And I kidnapped her. I've got her hidden away."

Hannah gasped. *Where? Tell him where,* she begged silently.

"I told Hannah she'll never see her mom again if she doesn't do what I tell her. She'll give me back the money."

The larger man frowned and brandished the huge gun. "You kidnapped your sick girlfriend? You're a real piece of work."

"Okay, listen, man." Sweat was running down Billy Joe's face and soaking the neck of his T-shirt. "Here's the deal. The drugs are hidden in the Toyota. But that bitch Hannah took it to town. She's got strict orders not to touch my damn car, but she took it anyway. Bet you can't guess where I put 'em. The drugs." Despite the gun pointed at him, Billy Joe's voice took on the bragging tone he used when he was sure he'd done something brilliant. "They're hidden in the trunk lining."

The man rolled his eyes and raised his gun.

"No, wait," Billy Joe begged. "I was trying something new. A better way to hide them for transport. I swear man, that's all. As soon as I made sure it worked, I was going to ask to show it to Mr. Ficone." Billy Joe took a nervous breath. "Or you. Maybe you'd want to see it first. You could take the credit for thinking it up if you want."

The man with the tattoo flexed his fingers around the handle of the handgun.

"Okay, listen. Hannah will be back any minute. She'd better be." He turned his hands palms out and continued babbling. "Wait till you see the car. It's brilliant, the way I hid the drugs. It's all fixed up, ready to go."

Fear and desperation twisted Hannah's heart. Billy Joe was off on his favorite subject. Cars. The moment when he might have revealed where her mother was had passed.

"It's a blue Toyota. Oh, I said that already. Anyhow, I painted it and boosted the engine. Th-the passenger-side mirror is broken and there's a crack in the windshield. It looks like any old family car on the outside, but under the hood is a screaming turbo-charged V-8. It's perfect for transport." Billy Joe had turned his body slightly to the right and was gesturing with his left hand to emphasize what he was saying, but Hannah saw him slowly reaching behind him to the waistband of his jeans.

"What about the money? I don't buy that your new guy or the girl—Hannah?—stole it."

"No, no. Listen. I swear. I'm giving you the real deal." Billy Joe's words tumbled over each other. "It's Hannah. That bitch is the key." He giggled. "The key. You'd better believe me. She's the one you want." He got his fingers wrapped around the handle of the gun that was stuck in his waistband and covered with his untucked shirt.

The man with the red tattoo stiffened and gripped his weapon tightly. "Don't move, slimeball!" the big man shouted.

"Look, I swear on my mama's life. Okay, so I kept those few drugs that are hid in the Toyota. But Hannah's the one who took the money. Not me. Make her talk. She's holding the key to everything," Billy Joe stammered.

Then, as Hannah watched in horror, he pulled out the gun. *No! Don't!* She covered her mouth with her hand to keep from screaming.

Billy Joe fired. The gun bucked in his hand and the bullet struck the garage wall at least three feet above the other man's head.

Without changing his position or his expression, the big man's finger squeezed the trigger. Billy Joe bucked once, then the back of his shirt blossomed with red, like ink in water. He made a strangled sound, then collapsed to the floor, right where he stood. The small gun he was holding dropped to the concrete with a metallic clatter.

Hannah tried to scream, but her voice was trapped behind her closed throat. The last thing she saw before she turned and ran toward Billy Joe's car was the big man's dark eyes on her and the gaping barrel of the gun pointed directly at her.

A LONG TIME later, Hannah wrapped her hands around the thick white mug, savoring its warmth. It was almost midnight—four hours since she'd watched a man shoot Billy Joe in the heart. In one sense it seemed as though it had happened to someone else. But then she would close her eyes and she was there, watching the blood spread across the back of his shirt like a rose blooming in fast-forward on a nature show.

He was dead. Billy Joe was dead, and the secret of where he'd taken her mother had died with him. A spasm of panic shot through her and her hand jerked, spilling the coffee. She grabbed a napkin from a chrome dispenser and laid it on top of the spilled liquid.

Ever since her mother had disappeared, Hannah had been imagining things. She knew her mother was not literally dead yet—not from her disease. But nightmar- ish images of where she was being held swirled con- tinuously in Hannah's mind.

She could be lying in a bed or on a pallet on a cold floor, her breathing labored, her paper-thin skin turning more and more sallow as the time since her last dialysis treatment grew longer. Without the life-giving proce- dure, the toxins that her diseased liver couldn't me- tabolize would kill her within days, if Billy Joe hadn't killed her already.

Her once-beautiful mother, still young at forty-two, was an alcoholic. She'd been as good a mother as she could be, given her addiction, while the liquor had sys- tematically destroyed her liver. By the time Hannah was sixteen, she had become her mom's caregiver.

Right now, sitting in the bright diner with the mug of hot coffee in her hands, she couldn't even remember how she'd gotten into Billy Joe's car, peeled out of the driveway or gotten on the interstate. Her only thought had been to run as if the hounds of hell were behind her. All she remembered was that desperate need to stay alive so she could find her mother.

A few minutes ago, four hours and almost two hundred miles later, she'd been forced to stop because she was about out of gas. She took a swallow of hot, strong coffee. What was she going to do? Go back to Dowdie, Texas, where Sheriff Harlan King was already suspicious of her and her mother? He'd been called twice in the past few months, once by neighbors and once by Hannah herself, complaining about her mom's and Billy Joe's screaming fights. Two years ago, he'd nearly busted her mom for possession of marijuana.

She thought about what he and his deputies would find this time. Her brain too easily conjured up a picture of Billy Joe, lying in a puddle of his own blood on the floor of the garage, her mother, missing with no explanation, Hannah herself gone, with brand-new tire skid marks on the concrete driveway, and who knew what kind of evidence of illegal drugs in the garage, on Billy Joe's body, even in her mom's house.

She couldn't go back.

The sheriff would never believe her. He'd arrest her and send her to prison and one day they'd find her mother's body in a ditch or a remote cabin or an abandoned car, and people in Dowdie would talk about Hannah Martin, who'd killed her mother and her mother's boyfriend, and how quiet and friendly she'd always seemed.

It was a catch-22. If she went back, all the sheriff's emphasis would be on her, and they probably wouldn't find her mother until it was too late. But if she didn't go back, then it might be days before anyone knew her mother was missing. Either way, she was terrified that her mom's fate was sealed.

She put her palms over her eyes, blocking out the restaurant's harsh fluorescent lights. She'd spent the past twenty-four hours begging Billy Joe to bring her mother back home. She'd sworn on her mother's life and her own that she wouldn't tell a soul, that she would do anything, *anything* he wanted her to, if he would only bring her mother back home so Hannah could take care of her.

But Billy Joe had been cold and cruel. He'd pushed her up against the wall of her bedroom and told her in explicit detail what he would do to her if she didn't *shut up.*

At that moment, Hannah had begun to devise a plan to follow Billy Joe to where he was holding her mother. But now, Billy Joe was dead.

Hannah's eyes burned and her insides felt more hollow and scorched than they'd ever felt before. Her mother was her only family, and she had no way to find her. Pressing her hand to her chest, Hannah felt the loneliness and grief like a palpable thing.

She picked up the mug and drained the last drops of coffee, then slid out of the booth and went to the cash register. A girl with straight black hair and black eye shadow that didn't mask the purplish skin under her eyes gave Hannah a hard look along with her change. "You want a place to sleep for a couple hours?" she asked.

Hannah shook her head.

"No charge. There ain't a lot of traffic tonight. I'll give you the room closest to here. You don't have to worry about anybody bothering you."

"Thanks," Hannah said, "but I've got to get to—" Where? For the first time, she realized she had no idea where she was going. Or where she was. "Where am— I mean, what town is this?"

The girl frowned. "Really? You don't know? Girl, you need some rest. You're about ten miles from Shreveport."

"Louisiana?" Hannah said.

The girl angled her head. "Yeah…. You sure you don't want to sleep awhile?" She paused for a second, studying Hannah. "You can park your car in the back. Nobody'll see it back there."

Hannah shook her head as she took her change. "Thanks," she said, giving the girl a tired smile. "That's awfully nice of you, but I'd better get going."

"Where you headed?"

Hannah stopped at the door and looked out at the interstate that ran past the truck stop, then back at the girl. She'd driven east, but she had no idea where she was going or what she was going to do when she got there. She had to have a plan before she went back to Dowdie. Otherwise all she'd accomplish would be to get herself arrested.

Shreveport, Louisiana. She wasn't quite sure where in the state Shreveport was, but there was one place in Louisiana she did know. Chef Voleur, on the north shore of Lake Pontchartrain.

She recalled a photo her mother had given her a long time ago. It was a picture of two young women, arm in arm, laughing. Her mother had always talked about Chef Voleur and her best friend. *We loved that place, Kathleen and me. That whole area around Lake Pontchartrain, from New Orleans to the north shore, is a magical place. She stayed, and I wish I had. Living there was like living in a movie.*

She made a vague gesture toward the road. "This is I-20, right?"

The girl nodded.

"I'm going to a town called Chef Voleur," she said. "To visit a friend of my mother's."

"You know you're going to get there around three o'clock in the morning, right?" the girl said dubiously.

Hannah waved a hand. "My mom's friend won't care."

Hannah prayed that her mother was right about the place being magical. Maybe things would be better there. They certainly couldn't get much worse. Could they?

As she walked back to Billy Joe's car, Hannah scanned the nearly empty parking lot, looking for the large maroon sedan that must have belonged to the man with the red tattoo, but she didn't see any sign of it.

Chapter Two

Just like the girl at the truck stop had predicted, Hannah wound up in Metairie at 3:00 a.m., unable to hold her eyes open any longer. She found a small, seedy motel that she figured wouldn't push the limit of her credit card, checked in and managed to sleep a little—in fits and starts, interrupted by nightmares of finding her mother just as she was breathing her last breath, or worse, leading the killer to her.

Around eight, she got up, showered and dressed, then sat down on the bed and dumped the contents of her purse. Like her mother, Hannah carried everything essential, valuable or meaningful in her purse. And like her mother, she wasn't sentimental, so most of the bag's contents were practical, except for two items. One was a photo her mother had given her years ago. The second was a sealed envelope.

Hannah picked up the envelope. With the traumatic events of the past couple of days, Hannah had totally forgotten about it. Looking at the words scrawled across the front made her want to break down and cry, but she didn't have time for that. So she carefully placed the envelope back in her purse and picked up her wallet.

She pulled the fragile, dog-eared photo out of a hidden pocket. It had to be thirty years old and was of her mother and Kathleen Griffin, her best friend. On the back it read, "Kath and me at her house." In a different hand was written "sisters forever," and an address in Chef Voleur, Louisiana.

Hannah looked up the address and took note of the directions. She was about to head out when her cell phone rang.

When she looked at the display, her heart skipped a beat. It was the Dowdie, Texas, sheriff's office. Hannah's already queasy stomach did a nauseating flip, the result of too little sleep, too much coffee and the image of Billy Joe's blood in her head.

She stared at the display, not moving, until the phone stopped ringing, then she dropped the phone back into her purse. There was no doubt in her mind why they were calling. They'd found Billy Joe's body. But how could she talk to them? What would she say? How would she explain to the authorities why she had run away to South Louisiana after witnessing a murder if she couldn't explain it to herself?

It took her about half an hour to drive to the address written on the back of the photo. It was across the street from a pizza place. With the photo in her hand she walked up to the building, hope clogging her throat.

A small voice deep inside her asked why she thought that talking to her mother's old friend would help her find and rescue her mother back in Texas.

She had no idea. Except that her only other choice was to trust Sheriff King to believe her, and she'd been taught at her mother's knee that authorities couldn't be trusted. Sheriffs. Police. Lawyers. They were the people who took children away from their mothers and placed them in foster care. They threatened sick people with prison for using marijuana to relieve the debilitating nausea associated with cancer and other diseases.

SHE KNOCKED ON the heavy wood door, then realized immediately that her tentative rapping probably couldn't be heard by anyone inside. So she rapped a second time, harder.

For a long moment that probably spanned no more than eight or ten seconds, she stood there listening and heard nothing. As she lifted her hand to rap again, she heard soft thuds on the other side of the door, as if someone was walking on a hardwood floor in socks or barefoot.

Standing stiffly, not quite ready to believe that she'd actually found her mother's best friend, Kathleen, she waited for the door to open.

When it did, it was not a pretty, dark-haired woman with even, striking features and a beautiful smile who stood there. It was a man. He was tall and lean and he had the same even, striking features but they were distorted in a scowl. And he had a cell phone to his ear.

After a brief, dismissive glance at her, he scanned the hallway behind her. Once he'd assured himself that she was the only one there, he said, "Hang on a minute," into the phone. "I've got to deal with somebody at the door." His tone was irritated and impatient.

Private investigator MacEllis Griffin kept his expression neutral as he eyed the young woman from the top of her streaked blond hair to the toes of her clunky sandals.

"What is it?" he growled. She stood there looking at him with all the apprehension of a kid called to the principal's office. Only she was no kid and he was no schoolteacher.

She could have been a kid. Her hair was pulled back

into a single messy braid that looked like she'd slept in it. The skinny jeans were slightly loose on her slender frame and the shirt looked more slept in than her hair.

"Hmm? Oh, nope. It's pretty slow here," Mack said into the phone as he tried to guess her age. Twenty-five? Twenty-six? Under twenty-five? Hard to tell. She had that heart-shaped face that always looked young. But faint blue circles under her eyes that matched the color of her jeans told him she was much older than her hair or clothes might indicate. She opened her mouth but he held up a finger. "Buono's working a missing person case," he said. "A seventeen-year-old. Probably ran away with her boyfriend."

"Well, get to the office and do something useful," Dawson Delancey, his boss, replied. "You could file your past three months' expenses if you're bored."

Mack didn't take his eyes off the young woman as he laughed. "I'll never be that bored," he said. "In fact, I might be real interested in something real soon." He smiled when the woman's gaze dropped from his and her cheeks turned pink.

"In what?" Dawson asked. "Was that the mailman delivering your latest issue of *Playboy?*"

"Right. He just got here from 2002," Mack responded. "Nope. Looks like I'm about to be hit up for Girl Scout cookies or a donation to a religious cause. I'd better go."

"I hope it's the donation. You don't need the cookies," Dawson said.

"Bite me," Mack said conversationally. "You're the one getting fat on your wife's Italian cooking."

"You're just jealous. Juliana and I will be back in Biloxi in a few days. I'll give you a call when we know for sure."

"Okay. Later. 'Bye."

As Mack hung up the phone, the young woman met his gaze and gave him a sad, self-conscious smile. The smile didn't reach her eyes and the only thing it accomplished was to make her look older and sadder.

A familiar sinking feeling gnawed at his stomach. He knew that smile. He'd never met this woman before, but he knew her type way too well. Standing there with that sadness in her eyes, that furrow between her brows. She was the embodiment of a lot of things he'd worked very hard to forget. She was exactly the type of person—the type of woman—he'd spent his adult life avoiding.

He upped his scowl by about a hundred watts and aimed it directly at her. With any luck, she'd turn and run. Her type was easily intimidated.

But her gaze didn't waver. She lifted her chin and to his surprise, he recognized a staunch determination in her green eyes, along with a spark of stubbornness. Interesting. But the small furrow between her brows didn't smooth out and the corners of her mouth were still pinched and tight.

He put his hand on the doorknob, preparing to close the door and get back to his coffee. "Can I help you?" he asked grudgingly.

"I'm looking for Kathleen Griffin," she said quietly.

The name hit him like a blow to the solar plexus. "Who?" he said, an automatic response designed to give him a second to think. But his brain seemed suddenly to be caught in a loop. *Kathleen Griffin, Kathleen. Kathleen.*

"K-Kathleen Griffin. The mailbox said Griffin." She gestured vaguely toward the front door.

It had been twenty years since his mother had died. This young woman wouldn't have been more than five or six at the time. Why would she be looking for his mother? "What's this about?"

"It's…personal," she said, glancing behind him into his foyer.

"I doubt that," he said flatly. "Go peddle whatever you're selling somewhere else. Kathleen Griffin doesn't live here." He started to close the door, but she held out a small, dog-eared photo. The paper was old and faded, but one of the two women in the picture looked familiar.

"Please," she said. Her hand was trembling, making the paper flutter.

"What's that?" he asked, knowing he was going to regret having asked that question. He held the door in its half-shut position.

The young woman's throat quivered as she swallowed. "It's a picture of my mother and Kathleen Griffin," she said, lifting her chin. "I really need to see her. It's a—" she bit her lower lip briefly and her gaze faltered "—it's a matter of life and death."

He gave a short laugh, but cut it off when she winced. "Life and death," he said dubiously. "Who are you?"

"Hannah Martin," she responded. "My mother is Stephanie Clemens."

She waited, watching him. But he didn't recognize the name. He gave a quick shake of his head, took a small step backward and started to close the door.

"You're her son, aren't you?"

Her words sent his stomach diving straight down to his toes. He shook his head, not in denial—in resignation. She had him and he knew it. He also knew that if he didn't do whatever he had to do in order to get rid of her this minute, he was going to regret it for a long time. "I'm sorry, but Kathleen Griffin is dead. So…" He put his hand on the door, preparing to close it.

"Oh. Oh, no," Hannah Martin said, her eyes filling with tears and her face losing its color. "I'm so sorry—" she started, but at that instant, her phone rang. She jerked at the sound, then reached into her purse and pulled it out.

As Mack watched, she looked at the screen as if she was afraid it might reach out and bite her. When she checked the display, her face lost what little color it had. She made a quiet sound, like a small animal cornered by a hungry predator. Her fingers tightened on the phone until the knuckles turned white, and all the time, the phone kept ringing, a loud, strident peal.

Whoever was on the other end of that call frightened her. In fact, she looked as if she'd seen a ghost. When the ringing finally stopped, Hannah dropped the phone back into her purse as if it were made of molten lava.

Mack had missed his best opportunity. He should have closed the door as soon as her phone rang. It was the perfect opportunity to escape. But he hadn't taken it. He wasn't sure why.

"I'm sorry about your mother," she said in a trembling voice. "I don't know what I was thinking, coming here. I apologize for bothering you." She closed her eyes briefly.

She'd let him off the hook. He took a step backward, preparing to close the door, because of course, she was about to turn and walk away.

But she didn't move. Her ghostly white face took on a faint greenish hue. She swayed like a slender tree in a punishing wind. Then she fainted.

Mack dived, catching her in time to keep her head from hitting the floor. She was fairly short, compared to his six-foot-one-inch height and he'd already noticed that she wasn't a lightweight. Her body was compact and firm. Lowering her gently to the floor, he grabbed a pillow off the couch and placed it under her head, making the decision to leave her on the floor rather than try to move her to the couch or a bed.

By the time he'd gotten the pillow under her head, she'd woken up. He recalled a paramedic telling him once that if someone passed out and woke up immediately, they were probably in no immediate danger.

Her face still had that greenish hue, although surprisingly, it didn't detract from its loveliness. He retrieved the photo she'd dropped when she'd passed out. He looked at the two young women—girls, really. They were both pretty and pleasant-faced. They were laughing at whoever was taking the picture, and behind them, Mack recognized the furniture. Most of it was still here. He knew one of the girls. It was his mother. He smiled sadly, seeing how young and happy and innocent she looked.

He'd never seen the other girl before, but the young woman lying just outside his door bore a strong resemblance to her. He turned the photo over. On the back was written "Kath and me at her house" in an unfamiliar hand. The other handwriting he knew. It was his mother's flowery script. She'd written "sisters forever" and his address.

Hannah stirred and tried to sit up. "What happened?" she asked, looking around in confusion.

"You fainted," he said.

She stared at him. "No, I didn't," she said, frowning at him suspiciously. "I never faint. Did you do something—?" But then her hand went to her head. "I feel dizzy."

"Just sit there a minute. I'll get you some water," he said grudgingly. He rose and drew her a glass of tap water. When he handed her the glass, she drank about half of it.

Then she shook her head as if trying to shake off a haze. "I guess I must have fainted."

"I guess," he said, a faint wryness in his voice.

She rose onto her haunches and stood, then grabbed on to his forearm for a second, to steady herself. "I never faint," she said again.

Mack smiled. "So I've heard," he said, thinking she was stubborn. He assessed her. Her color was still not good. "Do you want to sit down?" he asked, then felt irritated at himself for asking. Hell, she'd stood up on her own. So it was the perfect time for her to leave. And again, he'd missed his chance. And right there was one of the primary reasons why he didn't get involved with her type. She was obviously on some personal mission that would consume her life until she accomplished it. A certain clue—she'd driven all night without stopping except to get coffee and gasoline.

"Thanks," she said, and turned and headed, a little unsteadily, for the small dining table. He followed her.

She started to sit, then looked around.

"Here," Mack said, handing her the photo. "This what you're looking for?"

She took it. "Was this what we were talking about when I—" she gestured toward the front door.

"When you didn't faint?" He nodded, deciding for the moment not to remind her that she'd received a phone call that had scared her.

She held the photo in one hand and touched the faces of the two girls with a fingertip. "According to my mother, she and Kathleen Griffin swore they'd always be there for one another. *Sisters forever.*"

"And?" Mack said, working to sound disinterested,

even though he was becoming more and more fascinated by this pretty, determined young woman who had driven all night to find her mother's best friend.

"And—" She stopped, looking confused. Then she shrugged. "And, I don't know. I'm not really sure why I'm here. I just remember my mother talking about how much she and Kathleen loved Chef Voleur and how they had made that promise to each other."

She picked up her purse from the dining room table and stood, gripping the back of the chair to steady herself. "I'm truly sorry about your mother." She paused.

He nodded. "She died a long time ago," he said dismissively.

That was another reason he didn't like to be around women like her. Although Hannah was obviously in need of help and had pushed herself beyond her limits, right this minute her concern was for him and he didn't like that one bit.

She looked down at the photo, then up at him. "You look just like her," she said. "You have to be her son."

"MacEllis Griffin," he said, offering neither his hand nor any further explanation. "Call me Mack."

"Mack," she said, "I apologize for bothering you." She started to stand.

"Wait," he said. "What's this life-and-death emergency?" He bit his tongue, literally. But it was too late.

To his dismay, hope flared in her eyes. "I'm—not sure I should—"

"Why don't you tell me what's wrong." What the hell was happening to him? When had his mouth cut itself off from his brain? He was just digging himself in deeper and deeper. And why? Because a pretty woman had fainted in his doorway? No. It was because he had the very definite feeling that when she'd said *life and death,* she wasn't overstating the issue at all.

She sank back into the chair and casually picked up a business card from a small stack on the table. "MacEllis Griffin," she said. "D&D Security?"

"It's a private firm that takes on certain security issues," he said, watching her.

"Security—like night guards at office buildings?"

Mack sent her an ironic look. "No."

She frowned for a second, then eyebrows rose. "You're a private investigator?"

"You could use that term, although we don't take the usual divorce or spouse-tailing cases."

"What do you take?"

The faint hope he'd seen in her eyes grew, although she was still stiff as a board and tension radiated from her like heat.

"We've handled our share of *life-and-death* cases," he said.

Her eyes went as opaque as turquoise.

"Sorry," he said. "I can be a sarcastic SOB at times. Here's a quick rundown of me. I'm thirty-one years old. I've been with D&D Security for three years. I'm licensed as an investigator with the state of Louisiana. Now, will you tell me why you drove all night to find my mother?"

"How do you know I drove all night?" she asked.

"Your eyes are twitching and the lids are drooping. Headache and exhaustion, I'd guess. You're trembling, probably from too much coffee. You haven't combed your hair and your clothes smell faintly of gasoline. You must have spilled a little while you were filling up. How far have you driven?"

She shifted in her chair. "What are you, some kind

of Sherlock Holmes?" she asked drily. "Maybe you can tell me what I had for dinner last night."

He smiled. "You didn't eat dinner. You didn't stop until you were out of gas. You had a cup of coffee and nothing else. Then you didn't stop again until you got a motel room. You slept in your clothes, although you didn't sleep much. You couldn't stop thinking about whatever happened that frightened you so much that you took off without packing."

"How—?"

"If you'd packed, you'd have changed clothes." He stopped. "My question is, what or who are you running from?"

She opened her mouth to speak and then closed it again. He saw tears start in her eyes, but she blinked to keep them from falling. When she spoke, there was no trace of the tears in her voice. "I'm not running from anyone," she said, straightening her spine.

Mack knew from her voice that she was lying, and from her determined glare that she'd decided something. Probably to unload her woes upon him. He braced himself.

She stared at him for so long he was beginning to wonder if she'd fallen asleep with her eyes wide-open. But about the time he'd decided to snap his fingers in front of her face, she sat back with a sigh. "I drove here from Dowdie, Texas. Eight hours. And I've got to start back today. As soon as I can. My mother is—" She stopped as tears welled in her eyes. She wiped a hand down her face, then swiped at the dampness on her cheeks with her fingers.

"Your mother?" Mack said encouragingly.

"She's very ill. She has to have dialysis or she'll die." Mack waited, but she didn't say anything else. She pressed her lips together and clenched her jaw, doing her best not to cry.

"Do you need money?" he asked gently. "To pay for the treatments?"

"What? No! I don't need money. My mother has insurance."

"So why did you drive all this way just to turn around and go back?"

"It's complicated," she said.

"Most things are, especially if they involve running."

Tears welled again, and she pulled a tissue out of her purse and wiped her eyes. "I've kept that photo in my purse for years. Mom always told me that if I needed anything and she wasn't—wasn't—" She took a quick breath. "I should find Kathleen."

Mack's brows rose when she'd stumbled over her words. He pushed his chair back and stood. "Okay. Well, I'm Kathleen's son, so if you'll tell me what you need, I'll take care of it for you."

She played with the water glass, tracing a droplet of water up one side and down the other. "I can't tell you. It's too dangerous."

"Dangerous to who?" Mack asked.

"To my mother."

"Look," he said. "You need to start at the beginning. I can't figure out what you're talking about and I haven't heard anything that sounds dangerous yet, except your mother's illness. And you said she's getting dialysis."

"That's just it. She's not."

"Why not?"

"Because—" She sobbed, then banged her open palm on the table. "I can't stop crying."

Mack got up and refilled her water. He set it in front

of her and watched her as she drank it, hiccuped, then drank some more.

"Now. Why isn't she getting dialysis?"

"Because she's been kidnapped."

Mack flopped down in the chair. "Kidnapped? Is this some kind of joke?"

She stared at him, anger burning away the tears. "A joke? That's what you think?"

He opened his mouth then shook his head. He wasn't sure what he thought at the moment. He'd figured she *had* come to ask for money and it was just taking her a while to work up the nerve.

He studied her. Her skin was still colorless. She looked exhausted and terrified and so far she wasn't making a lot of sense.

"Okay. Your mother's been kidnapped. By who? Have they contacted you? Do they want a ransom? And have you talked to the police?"

"No! No. It's not that kind of kidnapping. And I can't go to—" She stopped talking.

Mack sighed. "Of course you can't. Why not?"

"They can't help. Nobody can help. I don't even know why I came here. I had to run. He was going to shoot me." She looked at the water glass. "I should have stayed," she said, her voice a mutter now. "I should have confronted him."

Well, she wasn't talking to him any longer.

"But there was all that blood," she continued. "And Billy Joe just collapsed and died. So I ran. I thought I had to save myself so I could find my mother before she died. But now she's going to die anyway. Oh, I don't know what to do."

"Whoa, damn it! Slow down." Mack did his best to put everything she'd said into logical order. If she wasn't just crazy, then she'd been through some kind of horrible trauma. "Hannah. Let's start over and take this slow. Who was going to shoot you? Whose blood did you see and who is Billy Joe?"

She stared at him for a moment, as if trying to figure out what he was doing there, in her reality. Then she blinked. "Oh." She shot up out of the chair and slung her purse strap over her shoulder. "I apologize," she said. "I think I've made a mistake." She looked at the business card in her hand, then stuffed it into her jeans pocket and ran out the front door.

"Hannah, wait!" he called. He started to run after her, but his protective instincts kicked in.

Good riddance, he thought when he heard the outside door slam. She had to have come here for money, then lost her nerve and tried to make up some kind of story. She'd never make it as a grifter. Her heart-shaped face gave too much away. He'd watched the kaleidoscope of expressions that flitted across her features as she'd listened to her cell phone ring. Bewilderment, fear, anger, resignation, each taking its turn, then the cycle had started all over again.

He felt sorry for her. *Whoa.* That was the kind of thinking that could get him into deep trouble, if he let himself get drawn in. He was lucky she'd run out when she did. Good riddance, indeed.

While his brain was congratulating him for dodging that bullet, he found himself rushing out the front door. She'd made it down his long sidewalk to her car, digging a large ring of keys out of her purse and unlocking a dark blue Toyota.

Mack used his phone to snap a shot of the rear of her car just as she climbed in. The license plate was from Texas. And even from half a block away, he could see two bullet holes in the bumper near the plate. Recent ones.

Maybe she hadn't been making it all up.

Although he had the snapshot, he jotted the license plate number down on a small notepad that he always carried. When he put the pad back into his shirt pocket, it seemed to burn his skin. He sighed. He was going to regret this.

No. That wasn't accurate. He already did. But even as he thought that, his mind had already latched on to the mystery of Hannah Martin. Kidnapping, murder, blood, pursuit, death.

"Who are you, Hannah Martin?" he muttered. "And why did you come to me?"

Chapter Three

Hannah drove straight from St. Charles Avenue to her motel in Metairie in an exhausted haze. But now, sitting in her parked car, her brain was whirling, replaying every second of the past hour.

What had possessed her to place all her hopes of saving her mother on an old photo of a friendship from more than thirty years before? All she'd done was exhaust herself driving and waste over twelve of the precious hours her mother had left before her body went into toxic liver failure. All she'd gained for her trouble was the not-so-sympathetic ear of Kathleen Griffin's handsome if grouchy son.

She turned off the engine and got out of the car. As soon as she put weight on her knees, they gave way. She barely managed to grab at the door frame to keep from falling. Her heart raced, her head felt weird—light and heavy at the same time—and the edges of her vision were turning black. It had to be exhaustion and hunger.

After a few seconds, she gingerly let go of the hot metal door frame and tested her ability to walk. Not too bad. But her hands trembled so much that it took her three tries to insert her key card into the motel's door.

Once she was inside with the door closed, the tears she'd been holding back ever since she'd watched Billy

Joe collapse and die came, as if floodgates had opened. She flopped down onto the bed and grabbed one of the pillows to hug as she cried. But within a couple of moments, she clenched her jaw and wiped her face.

That was enough of that. She didn't have time to cry. She had to figure out what she was going to do. Here she was, eight hours away from her home, and if someone asked her why she'd driven all that way, she wouldn't have been able tell them. In fact, she'd run away again as soon as Mack had started questioning her. He'd made her realize just how little she'd thought about what she was going to do.

What if she drove back to Dowdie and did what she should have done—gone to Sheriff King? For that matter, what if she'd gone to him about Billy Joe's obvious involvement in something illegal? Would things be completely different now? Would Billy Joe be in jail instead of dead and would her mother be safe and sound at home, preparing to go for dialysis later in the week?

Or would she and her mother be sitting in an interrogation room trying to explain to the sheriff that they knew nothing about what Billy Joe was or was not doing?

When she'd raced to the Toyota and taken off with Billy Joe's killer on her heels, she had actually considered going to the sheriff—for about ten seconds. Until she reminded herself that in her world, authorities like the police or Children's Services had the power to destroy her life.

From long ago when she'd been barely old enough to understand, her mother's admonitions were ingrained in her. *If you tell the police Mommy fell asleep with a cigarette and started a fire, they'll take you away from me and put you in an orphanage. You can put the fire out, can't you, sweetie? Just put it out and don't tell any-body. Then we'll be safe. We'll take care of each other.*

And they had. Her mother had raised her alone. It had been just the two of them against the world. Then, when the roles had become reversed as her mother's cirrhosis worsened, Hannah had taken care of her without regret—until the moment she'd witnessed a murder and run away.

Suddenly, Hannah remembered the phone call she'd gotten while she'd been standing outside Kathleen Griffin's apartment. She blotted her cheeks on her shirt-sleeve then fished inside her purse for her phone. Her fingers touched the smooth paper of the envelope, but she pushed it aside. Whatever was inside it wasn't going to help her right now. In fact, it might make things worse.

She found her phone and sat there holding it, not wanting to look at the display. Maybe she'd misread the caller ID. Maybe her exhausted mind had merely overlaid Billy Joe's name over whoever had really been calling her. But when she looked, the display definitely read "B.J." Her heart jumped, just as it had earlier.

Someone was calling her from Billy Joe's phone. There were only two possibilities. The man with the red tattoo, who'd shot Billy Joe in cold blood, or the sheriff.

As she'd peeled out of her mother's driveway in her haste to escape Billy Joe's killer, she'd prayed that the man would keep shooting at the Toyota until he'd emptied his gun. She'd prayed that one of their unconcerned neighbors would hear the shots and call the sheriff, and that the sheriff would catch him red-handed and charge him with Billy Joe's murder. And she'd prayed that everybody in town would become so wrapped up in the murder that they'd forget about Hannah Martin.

She accessed new voice mails. There were two. If it was the killer who had called her, had he really been dumb enough to leave a message? She skipped the message from the sheriff's office without listening to it and played the second incoming message.

"Where'd you go, Hannah?" She cringed and swallowed against a sick dread that settled in her stomach. That wasn't the sheriff. It was the man with the red tattoo on his hand. She'd never forget that awful voice as long as she lived.

"I know you don't want to talk to me, but I need to see you, talk to you. I need to make sure you're all right. Call me as soon as possible and let me know where you are. I'm worried about you. Bye-bye, Hannah."

Numbly, Hannah pressed the off button. She sat there, trying to will away the nausea that was getting worse with every passing second. Then, unable to stave it off any longer, she jumped up and ran into the bathroom, where she heaved drily. After a moment the heaves slowed, then stopped. She splashed water on her face over and over, trying to cool her heated skin and soothe her burning eyes.

At last the nausea dissipated, but there wasn't enough water in the world to wash away the sight of what that man had done to Billy Joe.

Had her mother's boyfriend deserved to die in such a horrible way? Maybe. Maybe not. But she wondered—if she'd gotten the chance to kill him, would she? She couldn't honestly deny it. Of course, she'd have tortured him first to find out where he was holding her mother.

When she'd come home from the drugstore with her mother's prescriptions only to find her missing, she'd threatened Billy Joe with going to the sheriff, but he'd quickly and effectively reminded her of his earlier warning.

She should have made good on her threat and gone to the sheriff then. She should have realized that of the two, Billy Joe or the sheriff, the sheriff was the more trustworthy. He'd have arrested Billy Joe and Hannah and her mother would be at home now, safe and healthy.

But instead she'd done the cowardly thing. She'd kept her mouth shut. She'd pretended nothing was wrong. It was what she'd always done. Long, harsh experience had ingrained the habit into her, as deeply as drinking was ingrained in her mother. It was what alcoholics did. It was what the children of alcoholics did. They pretended and lied and never told their secrets.

But now, doing what she'd always done was going to get her mother killed.

Hannah stood, grabbing the back of a chair when she felt light-headed. She needed to head back to Dowdie, but a lifetime of taking care of her mother and herself had taught her to pay attention to her body. There was no way she could drive eight hours tonight, no matter how desperate she was to get back home and find her mother. She'd fall asleep at the wheel.

Digging into her purse, she pushed aside the sealed envelope and her wallet, searching for the two high-energy protein bars she'd seen earlier. They were a little misshapen and the worse for wear, but still sealed. When she opened the first one, it was practically all crumbs, but she ate it anyhow, then ate the second one as well, washing them down with water from the tap in the bathroom, hoping that they'd be enough to satisfy her hunger and keep her from feeling so faint.

Then she took a shower, which made her feel a little

better, if she didn't count the exhaustion and her still queasy stomach.

Dressed in the only clothes she had, she lay down on the bed and turned on the TV, hoping to relax by watching a mindless sitcom for a while. It was five o'clock in the afternoon, according to the bedside clock. She groaned. It had been twenty-two hours since she'd witnessed Billy Joe's murder and run for her life. During that time, she hadn't closed her eyes, except for that fitful nap she'd taken early that morning.

She flipped channels until she recognized an episode of *Friends*. She leaned back against the pillows and tried to concentrate on the jokes Chandler was making. Four episodes later, she groaned and shifted position. She scrolled through the other channels on the old TV, but there was nothing interesting on. She reached for her paper cup of water, but it was empty, so she dragged herself up from the bed and went into the tiny bathroom to refill it. The next thing she knew, she'd dropped the cup and splashed water all over her legs and the floor. She'd fallen asleep standing up and dropped the cup.

She tossed a towel down and dried the water, but when she straightened, she started feeling queasy again. And now the edges of her vision were turning black and sparkly, which told her she'd faint if she didn't lie down.

She lay down on the bed. Was all this caused by her exhaustion and hunger? She'd eaten and rested— a little. She didn't have to consider for long to figure out that the nausea and light-headedness were the result of all the stress she'd been under added to hunger and weariness. Within the past forty-eight hours, her mother had been abducted from her house, her life and her mother's had been threatened and she'd witnessed the kidnapper—the only person who knew where her mother was—murdered in cold blood.

Then, panicked and thinking only of staying alive, Hannah had fled.

Breathing shallowly, Hannah waited for the nausea and light-headedness to pass. She closed her eyes and tried her best to relax and clear her mind. But Mack Griffin's slow, knowing smile rose before her closed lids.

During those first few seconds after he'd opened the door, she'd had the odd notion that her mother had sent her to Kathleen Griffin's home for this very reason. Because her own personal knight in shining armor had opened the door, ready and waiting to charge into battle for her, to rescue her mother and sweep them both away from harsh reality, pain and heartache.

But as soon as he'd fixed those hazel eyes on her, it had been immediately obvious that he had no idea who she was, nor did he care.

She should have turned and run sooner than she had, but at the time, she hadn't realized that with each passing second she'd become more mesmerized by his greenish-gold eyes and his large, capable hands and more dismayed that she was so affected by a perfect stranger. Still, in that first fairy-tale moment, something in his eyes behind the cynical smile and the worldly attitude had made her think he really could rescue her, even though she knew nothing about him except that he apparently was Kathleen Griffin's son.

He might look honorable and trustworthy and knight-like, but Hannah reminded herself of what she had learned at her mother's knee—men were *never* trustworthy. As big and strong and protective as they seemed, the reality was that men were always liars, bullies and cheaters.

But somewhere along the line her mother had gotten it wrong, because Stephanie also believed that women were weak. All they could do to protect themselves was pretend there was nothing wrong, lie when questioned and trust the untrustworthy men, since they had no other choice.

Well, not Hannah. She'd decided a long time ago that she would only trust herself. She hadn't met a man yet who could take care of her as well as she took care of herself and her mother. She lay down and tried to relax. She'd sleep for a couple of hours, then check out and get the car filled up so she could—

The car.

Her eyes flew open. *Oh, dear Lord, the car.* How had she forgotten about the car? Billy Joe's voice, filled with naive pride, came back to her. *My car. That's where the drugs are. They're hidden in the trunk lining.*

She sat up, her heart thumping wildly. She'd driven for eight hours in a car filled with drugs. A *stolen* car, as she'd discovered when she'd gone through the glove box and found that it was registered to a Nelson Vance, of Paris, Texas.

She couldn't drive the Toyota back to Dowdie. She couldn't drive it one more foot. She needed to abandon it and leave the motel. Now.

She closed her aching eyes as tears of exhaustion, frustration and hopelessness welled up. That meant she had to wipe down the car, inside and out, to get rid of her fingerprints, and take a cab to another depressing motel, then make arrangements to find another car or ride the bus back to Dowdie. And she had to start right now. She couldn't afford to sleep until she'd put miles between her and the Toyota.

She pressed her palms against her eyes, wishing she dared to set her phone's alarm and sleep—if only for a half hour.

As if prompted by her thoughts, her phone rang. Hannah's heart jumped into her throat and every muscle in her body went on full fight-or-flight alert. It was him again. The man with the red tattoo. The man who'd killed Billy Joe. She sat up straight, wringing her hands. Her chest tightened until she could barely breathe. She was afraid to answer and afraid not to. Cringing with dread, she pressed the answer button and put the phone to her ear.

"Hey, Hannah Martin," the dreadful menacing voice said.

Terror arrowed through her. She wanted to drop the phone and smash it, but her fingers clutched it tightly and she pressed her other hand against her chest as she waited to hear what he said. She shouldn't have answered. She should have let it go to voice mail so she'd have a record of what he said.

"Not talking? That's okay," the voice said conversationally. "I just wanted to let you know I'll be seeing you soon. Very soon. You've got something that Billy Joe promised us."

She didn't speak, wasn't sure she could. She pulled the phone away from her ear. She needed to record him if she could just find the record button.

"Wh-what are you talking about?" she rasped, hoping to keep him talking. Where was the stupid button? She pressed Menu, Settings, every button she could think of. Then finally, there it was. Memo Record. She jabbed it.

"You know what I'm talking about," the man was saying. "You ran off with Billy Joe's car and we need to get it. Why don't we meet and I'll trade you my brand-new car for that beat-up Toyota. Oh, and I can pick up that other little item, too, that Billy Joe gave you. I've got to say, Hannah, it'll be good to see you." The voice was barely audible, but Hannah heard every word. There was no mistaking the implied threat. "Now, remind me where you're staying."

"I don't know who you are and I don't have anything. Billy Joe didn't give me anything!" she cried. "Leave me alone!"

"Don't act all innocent, Hannah. Billy Joe was fighting for his life. Why would he lie? But you were there. You know what he said. He said you stole Mr. Ficone's money. He said you're the key to the missing money." He paused, but she didn't take the bait. She didn't answer.

"Hey, that's okay. I'll call you back once I get closer to you. I'm driving right now and I really shouldn't be on the phone. So I'll be talking to you later, once I get to that town. Watch yourself, Hannah. Don't make the mistake of lying. You'll end up like Billy Joe."

She gasped. "You killed him. I know you did. I saw you."

"Oh, Hannah, you really should try to control that imagination of yours." he said, his voice as gentle and sweet as a new father's. "Oh, by the way, your mom says hi. Bye-bye, now."

"Wait!" she cried. "You know where my mother is—?"

The line went dead. "Wait—please. No, no, no." She stared at the display. The icon indicated that the computer was recording. With a shaking finger, she stopped it.

Your mother says hi. That couldn't be true, could it? The man with the red tattoo couldn't know where her mother was. Only Billy Joe knew and the man had killed him.

She held her finger over the play button, but after a few seconds, she shuddered and dropped the phone into her purse. She couldn't listen to it again. Besides, he was lying about her mother. When Billy Joe told him he'd kidnapped her, the man had sounded surprised and shocked. Then Billy Joe had died right in front of him. No. He didn't know where her mother was. He couldn't.

Could he?

MACK DRUMMED HIS fingers on his kitchen table as he waited for the search results to show up on his tablet. He'd input "Stephanie Clemens, Texas." There were eleven Stephanie Clemenses in the state, apparently, not to mention all the Clemenses that weren't Stephanies and all the Stephanies that weren't Clemenses.

He'd found one whose age was about right in a town called Dowdie. She was listed as forty-two years old and living with Hannah Martin, age twenty-five. Mack sat back in his chair, staring at the screen. So Stephanie Clemens was his odd visitor's mother. She was forty-two, which meant she'd been seventeen when her daughter was born. Mack shook his head. *Children having children.*

There was a telephone number listed beside Stephanie Clemens's name. He entered the number into his cell phone under the name Hannah Martin. Then he dialed it. There was no answer. Probably a landline.

He input Stephanie Ann Martin Clemens, Dowdie,

Texas, into a search engine, and three police reports popped up. The first, dated two years previously, was a call regarding drug activity at her home address. Mack skimmed the short paragraph. No arrests. Clemens claimed she used marijuana to alleviate nausea from an illness. Although she couldn't produce a doctor's order or even a note confirming that, the police hadn't placed her under arrest.

The second and third calls were for domestic disturbances. The location was the same address, but were four and five months before. They involved Clemens and Billy Joe Campbell, age thirty-eight. One of the calls had been made by Hannah Martin.

Mack typed in Hannah Martin, Dowdie, Texas, but found no other references to her. He sat, staring out through the French doors that opened onto the small patio behind his house. St. Charles Avenue, but what he saw wasn't a big concrete fountain and fish pool, it was Hannah. He should have known the instant he'd laid eyes on her that she'd be trouble. He should have recognized the signs.

"Two domestic disturbances involving your mother and her boyfriend," he said aloud. "That's been your life, hasn't it, Hannah? Watching your mother get beat up by thugs that didn't deserve her. She's the only role model you've ever had, isn't she? That's all you've ever known!" His voice gained in volume as anger built inside him.

Suddenly, the house was too small and hot for him. He vaulted up out of his desk chair, sending it crashing into the kitchen counter behind him. Then he threw open the French doors and stepped outside, gulping deep breaths of the cool breeze that had blown in with an afternoon thunderstorm. It was unusual for a summer storm to cool the air, but he wasn't complaining. After a few moments, the pressure in his chest and the heat along his scalp dissipated.

Mack knew too much about women like Stephanie Clemens and Hannah Martin. And he knew *way* too much about abusive boyfriends. He'd been six years old the first time he'd seen blood dripping from his mother's nose. Her boyfriend had slammed her face against one of the tall columns of the four-poster bed. Mack had flung himself at the guy, trying to break *his* nose, but at six, he wasn't strong enough or tall enough.

The jerk had swatted him away like a bothersome fly, then bent down to whisper in his ear, "If you try that again, your mom will hurt worse. Understand?"

Mack's hands cramped and he looked down to find that he'd clenched his fists. Carefully, he relaxed them, shaking them a little to ease the cramping. He took a few more breaths of chilly air, letting it flow through him, cooling the frustrated anger.

He found himself once again wishing Billy Joe Campbell were alive, because he'd like to have a few minutes with him, just long enough to give him a taste of his own medicine. But Mack had more sense than that, and more self-control—and Billy Joe was dead. He took one more deep breath, filling his lungs with the scent of damp earth and fresh rain, then went back inside.

As he was retrieving his chair and rolling it back up to the table, his phone rang. He looked at the display and sighed. It was Sadie, the woman he'd been seeing. "Hello," he said, making sure his voice was bland.

"Hey," Sadie said. "What happened to 'hi, doll,' or 'sexy Sadie'?"

"Busy," he said impatiently, not really trying to mask

the frustration in his voice. He looked at the clock in the corner of the screen.

"Well, business can wait until tomorrow. I'm back in town and I want to see you," Sadie said in her low, sexy voice. "Come over."

Mack arched his neck. It was easy to get too big a dose of Sadie. And he'd gotten a nearly lethal overdose about the time she'd gone out of town. Her absence had convinced him that he'd had enough of her to last a lifetime. He'd told her from the beginning that he wasn't interested in anything long-term, and she'd responded that she wasn't, either. As he rubbed his eyes, he wondered if she'd been telling the truth.

"Can't," he said. "I'm working on a new case and I'm pretty sure I'm going to be tied up for quite a while."

"Oh, come on," Sadie said. "You have to eat. Let's grab dinner and—"

"Sadie," he interrupted, gently but firmly. "No."

"Fine," she said. "Tell me about this big case you can't tear yourself away from."

"It's not just the case," he said. "It's a lot of things. It's been fun, but…"

"But?" she echoed.

"You know. We talked about this. We were never in it for the long haul. We both agreed."

There was a slight pause. "That's true."

He didn't speak. He really didn't like this. He wasn't quite sure why he'd chosen tonight as the night to break up with her.

"Okay, then," she said. "I enjoyed—everything."

"Me, too," he replied. He took a breath to say something else, but she hung up. He winced. That abrupt hang up was the only indication that she might have been upset.

Maybe he should have handled that in person, but unfortunately, Sadie could be quite persuasive in person. Or at least she had been once, he amended, as his brain compared Sadie and Hannah. Hannah, with her unmade-up face and flyaway hair and no lipstick, won by a mile.

Mack shook his head and resisted the urge to pound on his temples with his fists. He didn't want Hannah Martin in there. She was nothing but trouble. Mack had always loved women, but he'd learned very young that relationships were not for him. Whenever he met someone he was attracted to, he made his position clear from the first moment. If the woman protested at all, then she was not the woman for him. Most women he asked out were happy with the arrangement, because Mack was very careful to pick like-minded women. Usually he picked well. After a while, by mutual agreement, he and the woman parted ways and eventually he met another like-minded woman.

He sat down to send an email to Dusty Graves, Dawson's computer wizard, to ask how much longer until she had information back on the license plate of the car Hannah had been driving. As he did, his phone rang. Surely it wasn't Sadie again. *Give it up, doll.*

But when he looked, the display name was Dust007. "Hey, Dusty, what you got for me?"

"Finally got the info on that plate you wanted me to run," Dusty said, "but you're not going to like it."

"Why not?"

"It's registered to a Nelson Vance, of Paris, Texas. He reported it stolen about a week ago. The license and registration also report the vehicle as sky blue, not dark blue."

Mack's stomach sank. Stolen *and* repainted? Ten to

one, whoever stole it was either reselling cars or running drugs. Either way, this wasn't good. "A witness? Any sightings by highway patrol? Anything?"

"The Tyler, Texas, police have a BOLO out on the car. The DEA has been watching a small-time narcotics distribution ring operating around the area. The perps apparently steal a vehicle from a neighboring town or county, use it for one drug delivery, then clean it out and abandon it. This vehicle is suspected to have been stolen by the ring."

Dusty was right. Mack didn't like what he was hearing at all. What was Hannah Martin doing driving a car suspected of being stolen by a narcotics distribution ring?

Chapter Four

"What kind of narcotics do they deal in?" he asked Dusty.

"Mostly Oxy," Dusty said.

Stunned, Mack muttered a curse. *Oxycontin.*

"Yeah," Dusty continued. "Word is, they're bringing it into Galveston from Mexico. Get this. The DEA knows all about a big-time trafficker named Ficone in Galveston, but they've been spending their time watching a suspected small-time operator, until he was murdered yesterday."

"Murdered?" Dread settled heavy as an anvil in Mack's chest. "Yesterday? Who was he?"

"Campbell. Billy Joe Campbell. He was shot once in the chest at close range. A neighbor complained about gunshots." Dusty took a breath. "You know something about this?"

Hannah's jumbled words echoed in Mack's ears. *I had to run. He was going to shoot me.*

"Where did this happen?" he croaked, positive he knew the answer.

"Hang on."

Mack heard computer keys tapping.

"A little town called Dowdie." Dusty paused for a

second. "Mack, tell me you don't have a client who's driving that chopped car. That would not be good."

"Nope. No client. Just checking for a friend." Not a complete lie.

"O-kay," Dusty said, her tone making it obvious that she didn't believe him. "You want me to send you the details from the police report?"

"Yeah. Everything you've got on Billy Joe Campbell. I appreciate it."

"No problem, Mack. You be careful. I'll TTYL. 'Bye."

Mack hung up, remembering the changing expressions on Hannah's face and the terror in her eyes when her telephone rang. He knew that terror, knew it intimately. Had Hannah done what Mack hadn't been able to do when he was twelve? Had she killed the man who had hurt her mother?

He waited impatiently, repeatedly checking for new mail until Dusty's message about the murder came in. He scanned the police report, his heart sinking with every sentence. A neighbor had called the sheriff's office around 7:00 p.m. complaining about gunshots at 1400 Redbud Lane, Dowdie, Texas.

A sheriff's deputy arrived at around seven-thirty to find the house and driveway empty. A quick investigation by the deputy turned up a body of a white male, mid to late thirties, in the garage. Cause of death, a single gunshot wound to the chest. The victim was identified as Billy Joe Campbell of Fort Worth, Texas. The police report indicated that neither the owner of the house, a Ms. Stephanie Clemens, nor her daughter, Ms. Hannah Martin, could be found. Both were being sought for questioning in the matter.

Campbell had been killed around twelve hours before

Hannah had turned up at Mack's door, looking for Kathleen Griffin. She'd also mentioned seeing Billy Joe collapse and die and being shot at. What were the odds that Hannah had witnessed her mother's boyfriend being murdered?

A LOUD CRASH and a harsh male voice startled Hannah out of a restless sleep. Her pulse drummed in her ears and she couldn't catch a full breath. "Mom?" she called, before she came fully awake.

The crashing began again. With a start, she remembered. It couldn't be her mom. Her mom had been kidnapped by Billy Joe and Billy Joe was dead.

Hannah rubbed her eyes as she forced her brain to sort out the noises that were battering her ears. It had to be the man with the red tattoo. He'd found her.

"Police! Open up!"

Police? Surprised and terrified, Hannah jumped out of bed and ran to the door. "What is it? Did you find my—" She stopped herself just as she was about to throw the dead bolt. What if it wasn't the police?

She glanced at the clock on the bedside table. It was almost one o'clock in the morning. She'd slept for a couple of hours. "I need proof you're the police." She made her voice as stern as she could, but it still quavered.

"Hannah Martin, I'm Detective Anthony Teilhard of the Metairie Police Department. I've got the motel's night manager here. He's going to unlock the door and we're coming in. I'd suggest you move back."

She scrambled backward as a key turned in the doorknob and then in the dead bolt. The door swung open and slammed against the wall as three officers burst into the room, guns at the ready. Hannah shrieked as two of them, one male and one female, turned their weapons on her. The third officer quickly checked the bathroom and the tiny closet.

"Clear," he said.

The officer who'd entered first took three steps forward and looked down the barrel of his gun at her. "Hannah Martin?" he said.

Hannah's head jerked in a nod. Her first instinct was to retreat, but she bumped her hip on the corner of the bedside table. She was trapped between the bed and the wall. "Who—wha—?" Nothing but broken, senseless sounds escaped her constricted throat. She clutched at the neck of her shirt with trembling fingers.

"I'm Detective Teilhard. Keep your hands where I can see them. Good. Now, where did you get the car, Hannah?"

"The car?" she parroted. "It's—I don't—" All she could think about was Billy Joe saying, *That's where the drugs are. They're hidden in the trunk lining.*

"Come on, Hannah. Pull yourself together. You're in a lot of trouble. The best thing you can do is answer my questions. Now tell me about the car."

"I don't know anything," she said. It wasn't exactly true.

"Nothing?" Teilhard said wryly. "Okay, Hannah. In that case, looks like we're going to have to do this down at the station. You're under arrest for possession of a stolen vehicle, driving a stolen vehicle and transporting a stolen vehicle across state lines."

She waited, her heart in her throat, but he didn't mention illegal drugs or homicide.

The detective looked at the female officer. "Officer Waller, would you check her for weapons and cuff her, please?"

"Arms straight out at your sides, please," Officer Waller said.

Hannah obeyed, feeling a profound relief that the police were here about the car and not about Billy Joe's murder. When she caught Teilhard gazing at her with a puzzled look, she ducked her head and tried to compose her features. Had he seen the relief on her face?

The female officer started to pat her down. Hannah recoiled. "No, wait," she said quickly. "Please. I didn't know it was stolen. I'll tell you what I know. You don't have to arrest me." She felt a lump growing in her throat. If they arrested her, how was she ever going to get back to Dowdie to find her mother?

She swallowed hard, trying to stop the tears. She was sure Teilhard wasn't the type who could be swayed by a damsel in distress. In fact, his mouth was already thinning in a line of distaste at her hedging.

She needed to figure out what to do and fast, because it wasn't going to take the detective long to find out what she already knew—that the person who had stolen the car was dead, murdered, and that the car was filled with drugs. Then what would he do? He'd put her in jail. No question about it. She'd be charged with grand theft auto and murder. That meant that her mother would surely die.

Officer Waller quickly and efficiently finished patting her down, then pulled her arms behind her back and cuffed her hands.

"Do you really have to do this?" Hannah asked as the cold metal bit into her wrists, desperate to try anything to get out of being arrested. Anything but telling the truth. She was in too deep. If she tried to explain, Teilhard would laugh as he threw her into lockup. "It's got to be a misunderstanding. I apologize for the trouble. I mean, I thought I was borrowing my mom's boyfriend's car. Can't we just give the car back to its owner? I'll pay for any damages." She made her voice sound hopeful.

She could pretend all she wanted, but she knew that there was no way any sheriff's office or police station would send three armed officers to bring in one relatively harmless female driving a stolen car. This had to be about something else. Then a horrible thought occurred to her. Had her mother been found—dead? Were they really here to arrest her for two murders, Billy Joe's and her mother's?

Teilhard laughed. "Yeah. It's a misunderstanding," he said sarcastically. "Why'd you go to the trouble to repaint the car when you didn't bother to change the license plate or replace the broken passenger-side mirror? Kind of amateurish for a car thief. But it certainly narrows the suspect pool." He turned toward the door. "Let's go. I don't have time to stand around all day listening to 'he's my mom's boyfriend' and 'I didn't know.'" The last was said in a tinny falsetto. The other two officers laughed.

Hannah wanted to cry as she felt the last droplets of hope drain from her heart.

They put her in the back of the squad car and drove to the Metairie Police Station. Waller and Teilhard were in the car with her. The third officer had taken her key to drive the Toyota to the impound lot.

After several intensely uncomfortable minutes as she tried to keep her hands from going to sleep and her wrists from being permanently marked by the tight metal cuffs, they arrived. She was pulled out of the car and marched into the police station, handcuffed like a common thief. Officer Waller stood her in front of the booking counter in view of all the other officers, detectives and criminals, with the cuffs hurting more after the ride, while Teilhard got the forms filled out. Then he turned to her.

"I'm placing your purse in this plastic bag to be held until your release or until someone posts bail. Officer Waller?" He turned to the female officer.

"Yes, sir," Waller said, stepping forward.

"Please remove her earrings," Teilhard said, nodding toward Hannah. "Hannah, do you have any other jewelry? Piercings? Any prosthetics like a partial bridge in your mouth?" he asked.

She shook her head.

"Sir?" Waller said to Teilhard. "Do you want a full search?"

Teilhard assessed Hannah, then shook his head. "I don't think that will be necessary." He turned to a cop who'd been waiting at the counter. "Put her in one of the interrogation rooms and get her some coffee if she wants."

Hannah shook her head, but neither one of them paid any attention to her.

The cop took her into a small, stark room. "I'll get that coffee," he said and left.

She stood there next to the wooden table, not wanting to try sitting again with her hands cuffed behind her. As hard as it had been to sit in the police car with its upholstered backseat, a hard-backed chair would be torture.

She tried to take her mind off her aching shoulders and stinging wrists by studying the Formica tabletop. It was old and chipped, and had names and phrases carved into it. Idly, she wondered where Tony or Eddie Jewels or Turk had gotten their hands on something sharp enough to use to carve those deep grooves. She spent a few moments trying to read some other names and phrases, but her eyelids kept drooping.

The young officer came back with a cup of coffee that he set down on the table. He gestured toward it. "Sit," he said as he sat and drank a swallow from his cup.

Hannah tilted her head. "Do you think you could—"

For a moment, he stared back, bewildered, then she saw the light dawn in his eyes and he took a key from his pocket and undid her cuffs.

She sat, rubbing a red streak where the metal of the cuffs had pressed into her skin. Once she was seated again, she took a sip of the lukewarm liquid, which, although it was nearly transparent, still managed to taste burned. She drank the awful stuff, though, because she was thirsty and maybe the caffeine would keep her from giving in to the sleepy haze that was threatening to overtake her. When Detective Teilhard opened the door, she jumped and realized that she'd dozed off.

The officer stood and Teilhard took his place at the table. After nodding toward the two-way mirror and adjusting the position of the microphone, then making a short statement of date, time and individuals present, he spoke directly to Hannah.

"So, Hannah, we talked a little bit earlier about the car you were driving, didn't we?"

"Yes," she said.

"And we established that the car had been stolen and repainted."

"That's what you told me."

"Could you repeat for the record what you told *me* about the car?"

Hannah frowned at him. "All I know is that I thought it belonged to my mom's boyfriend."

He sighed audibly. "Could you be a little more specific?"

"Nobody told me it was stolen. It showed up at the house on—"

"I said, be specific, please," Teilhard said. "Who brought the car to the house and where exactly is the house?"

Hannah recounted what he'd asked her to. She was careful not to say Billy Joe's or her mother's names, but to refer to them as "my mother" and "her boyfriend."

Detective Teilhard drummed his fingers on the Formica table as Hannah talked. As tired and sleepy as she was, Hannah knew what he was doing. He was trying to make her nervous—trying to make her slip up and say something she didn't intend to say.

He continued drumming his fingers after she'd finished. Then he leaned forward. "Who's Billy Joe Campbell, Hannah?"

She started. The detective's silence while she'd talked had lulled her into a false complacency. Judging by the twinkle in Teilhard's eyes, that was exactly what he'd wanted.

"Billy Joe?" she stammered. "That's my mother's boyfriend."

"The one whose car you took?"

She lifted one shoulder.

"What happened to him?"

Hannah didn't have to work very hard to appear confused and worried. "What happened to him? I don't—" She paused but Teilhard didn't jump in. He let the silence stretch out.

Hannah clasped her hands in front of her and looked Teilhard straight in the eye. "It's something bad, isn't it?"

Teilhard assessed her. "You know the answer to that."

She nodded to herself, wondering how long she would have to keep up the pretense. How long she *could.* As tired as she was, she was afraid she might drift off to sleep while talking. If she did, she might mutter the truth. Her palms were clammy and her chest felt as if it were being squeezed in a vise.

"What are you trying to tell me?" she asked as the sight of Billy Joe's shirt blossoming with blood rose in her mind. "He's dead, isn't he? I can tell by the way you're looking at me."

Teilhard's dark eyes sparkled. "That's right, but you already knew that, didn't you? Come on, Hannah. Save us both some time, will you? Just tell me what I need to know."

Hannah started to cry, even though she knew it would alienate Detective Teilhard. She couldn't help it. She shouldn't have been surprised. She'd been fighting tears off and on ever since that instant when the bullet had exploded out of Billy Joe's back and his blood had spattered the panes of glass in the garage door. The tears poured down her face, pushed out because of everything that was bottled up inside her.

"Why'd you kill him, Hannah? Did you get tired of him whaling on your mom?"

"That's what you think?" she said, her voice going shrill. "You think I killed him?" She laughed and brushed tears off her cheeks, doing her best to stop crying. But she couldn't. Teilhard wasn't at all moved, but she was too far gone to stop.

"Well, if you didn't, then who did? Tell me. Was it your mom?"

"No!"

"Where is your mother? I haven't seen any sign of her at the motel or in the car. I understand she's quite ill. Did you leave her there in Dowdie, Texas, to face the music alone?"

"No. Of course not. I'd never leave her. I—"

"You what, Hannah? Tell me. I know you want to. It would make you feel so much better to just tell the truth."

"You don't understand. My mother is—too sick—" Hannah stopped. If she wasn't careful, she'd say too much. She pressed her lips together and tried to calm her throbbing pulse. "You have to believe me. I don't know who killed Billy Joe."

That much was true. She'd seen the man, but she had no idea who he was. For a moment she let herself imagine telling Teilhard the whole truth. The truth about Billy Joe and the drugs. About her mother, grievously ill and missing. And about the man with the red tattoo who shot Billy Joe in the heart, thereby stealing Hannah's only chance to find her mother in time to save her.

But Teilhard was smiling at her. A predatory smile, like the one the crocodile had shown Captain Hook. He was so anxious for her to confess that he was practically rubbing his hands together with glee. Obviously, she couldn't trust him.

After a moment, he spoke again. "Come on, Hannah. Tell me about Billy Joe and I'll put you up in a really nice hotel. I know you're tired. I know you want this to end."

Of course she wanted the interrogation to end. She was tired of crying, tired of lying, tired of listening to the detective's voice. She was just plain tired. Too tired to think straight. Too tired to hold her head up. "I can't tell you anything else," she said dully.

Teilhard narrowed his eyes. "Why did you come here? Were you hoping to establish an alibi here while somebody took care of your problem boyfriend for you?"

She stared at him. "What is wrong with you? I told you, I didn't kill him! And he's not my boyfriend. He's my mom's."

"Then why did you steal his car and run?"

She shrugged, as much to herself as to him. What if she told him? How much worse could it get? All she had to do was describe the killer to the police and tell them what she'd seen. Then they'd go after him and catch him, and she could be free to concentrate on finding her mother.

If they believed her.

But the man who'd shot Billy Joe had looked like a professional, and she'd seen enough television to know that professional killers didn't make mistakes. By the time the police went to her garage, would Billy Joe's body even be there? Or would the big man with the red tattoo have removed it and cleaned up every single bit of evidence, leaving nobody to blame for the murder except her?

She'd also seen the true-life horror stories of people being falsely accused of crimes and spending years in prison trying to prove their innocence. No. The lesson she'd learned from a lifetime of taking care of her alcoholic mother was still her safest bet. *Never tell your secrets. Never trust anybody.*

"Hannah? Why did you run?" Teilhard leaned forward. "I promise you I'll pull in every favor I've got to get you a deal if you'll just tell me what really happened."

"A *deal?* You're going to get me a *deal* for murdering

my mother's boyfriend? I did not kill him." The words scraped her dry throat as exhaustion enveloped her in a sleepy haze. "All I want to do is get out of here. I've got to get back home—to my mother." She stopped. She was saying too much. She waved a hand in a dismissive gesture. "I'm tired. I can't think straight."

"Of course you're tired, Hannah," Teilhard said. "Tired and hungry. Me, too. But I need the truth. That's all. It's simple. Just tell me what happened."

Hannah felt like her body and her mind were shutting down. She hardly understood a word Teilhard had said. Her stomach churned emptily, the protein bars long gone. Her head ached and the sparkly darkness was gathering at the edge of her vision again. She was almost past caring what happened to her.

Teilhard rocked backward in his chair and yawned and stretched.

Hannah tried not to yawn in response to his, but she couldn't suppress it. "I need sleep," she muttered, thinking if she had to sit upright much longer she'd faint.

Teilhard sighed. "Okay, Hannah. I've been patient. I've been helpful. I was hoping you and I could get this all straightened out. But…I'll tell you what. I'm going to give you overnight to think about what you want to tell me."

She roused a bit. "Not in here. I can't stay in here overnight!"

Teilhard perked up. "You won't have to if you talk," he said.

She rubbed her temples, regretting her outburst. She needed sleep. Until she could get some rest, she was incapable of making a decision. Incapable of thinking rationally. Incapable of figuring out how to find her mother. "I can't think. Have to sleep," she muttered.

The detective sighed. "Okay. But tomorrow morning, they're going to call you for arraignment for grand theft auto. At that point, it's probably going to be too late for me to pull any strings to help you. Do you understand what that means?'

Hannah closed her burning eyes.

"It means if you're arraigned for Billy Joe Campbell's murder, you're on your own. You can't depend on me or anyone else to help you."

She shrugged. "That's nothing new," she muttered.

"Fine!" Teilhard snapped and vaulted up, sending the wooden chair scraping across the bare floor.

She jumped and frowned at him in confusion.

"You're on your own. I'll find you a place to sleep and we'll talk again tomorrow."

She almost cried in relief. *A place to sleep.* It sounded like heaven.

Teilhard called for a female officer. When she arrived, he told her, "Please escort Miss Hannah Martin to the tank." He sighed. "I've got to wake up one of the prosecutors."

"The tank?" Hannah echoed as the female officer pulled her to her feet and led her out the door. "What's that?" But no one answered her question.

The officer guided her through the big room filled with desks and computer stations to the back of the building. When she opened the large metal door, Hannah saw the row of barred cells. She led Hannah past an empty cell to one that held two women.

The shorter, younger one wore a crotch-high skirt, over-the-knee boots, silver hair and silver eye shadow. The other woman had been crying. There were black streaks down her face and splotches on her sleeve from her mascara.

The officer opened the cell door. "Get in there," she said, not unkindly.

Hannah looked at the open cell door, then at the officer, then stepped through the door into a world like none she'd ever seen. The room was painted a no-color gray. The floors were tiled in a color that almost matched the walls and a metal bench. An old water fountain hung from the wall.

She took a long drink from the fountain. The water tasted of chlorine, but the chill soothed her burning stomach. She blotted her mouth with her fingers and sat on the end of the bench, as far away from the other women as she could get She moved around, trying to get comfortable as tears began to burn her eyes. She moaned involuntarily. "What's up with you in here, Miss Uptown Girl? I *know* you got somebody to call," the silver-haired woman said.

"Call?" Hannah repeated.

"Didn't you get your phone call?"

She shook her head.

"That ain't right," the woman mumbled. "Everybody s'pose to get a phone call."

Hannah shrugged, too tired and miserable to care about anything but closing her eyes. She looked sidelong at the two women. Silver Hair was peeling silver nail polish off her nails. The crying woman folded her arms and turned sideways on the bench, leaning against the wall.

Hannah copied her and found the position less uncomfortable than trying to sit straight.

"First time, sugar?" Silver Hair asked kindly. "You'll get the hang of it eventually."

"Dear Lord, I hope not," Hannah murmured.

Chapter Five

The next morning, an officer came for her and deposited her in another interrogation room. Desperately tired, she folded her arms on the table and dozed until Detective Teilhard came in, slamming the door behind him.

"Hannah, we need to talk about the vehicle you were driving."

She forced her burning eyes open to stare at him, thinking about what the silver-haired woman had said the night before. "I want my phone call."

"You haven't had your phone call yet?" The detective feigned surprise.

She straightened, wincing at the stiffness in her back. "No, I haven't."

Teilhard's mouth flattened, but he nodded. "Okay. If you say so." He nodded toward the mirrored wall where a phone was mounted next to the mirror.

She stood and stepped over to the phone, lifting the receiver from the cradle. Then she looked back at him. "Privacy, please?"

He got up. "I could use some more coffee."

Hannah lifted her hand, then realized she was about to punch in her mother's number. With a strong arrow of pain piercing her chest, she remembered that her mother wasn't at home. She was somewhere alone and sick and wondering why Hannah hadn't found her.

But there was no one else, unless she called Mack Griffin. Hadn't he handed her a card? Her hand went to the front pocket of her jeans. The female officer who had patted her down hadn't noticed it. She dug it out and looked at it. It was like him, actually. Deceptively simple and starkly elegant, yet completely self-contained. And completely uninterested in her.

She dialed his number, wondering if he would help her.

MACK WAS DRINKING coffee and checking his email when his cell phone rang. He answered distractedly as he scanned Dawson's message inviting him to a dinner party three weeks from the coming Saturday, at the Delancey Mansion in Chef Voleur. He'd probably have to go by himself, since he'd broken up with Sadie.

A tentative voice spoke in his ear. "Mack Griffin?"

Hannah. Mack sat up straight and glanced at the display. The number was a local one, a Metairie exchange. He gave himself a second to decide how to answer. Somehow he'd known he hadn't heard the last of her. He felt a slight loosening of his neck muscles. He realized he was relieved to hear from her.

"Yep," he said, as a frisson of worry took the edge off his relief. "What's going on, Hannah? You don't sound so good."

"It's been a long night," she responded, then, after a pause, "Could you—I mean would you be able to come to the Metairie Police Department? They took my car and kept me here all night and—" Her voice cracked a little.

He wasn't surprised, after what Dusty had told him

about the stolen car, especially since it was suspected to be involved in a drug distribution ring. He was, however, curious. The question still remained whether she'd known about the drugs. He looked at his watch. 8:15 a.m. He never scheduled an appointment before 10:00 a.m. so running over to Metairie for an hour or so wouldn't interfere with his day. Well, except that he'd have to drink his second cup of coffee on the road.

"I'll be there in twenty minutes. In the meantime, don't talk to anybody. Tell them you called your lawyer."

"But I haven't. I don't even know—"

"Hannah? Just tell them. I'll be there soon." Mack hung up and threw on a pair of slacks and a pale yellow dress shirt and headed downstairs to his car. He made it to Metairie in under twenty minutes and into the police station from the parking lot within another three. He told the officer at the desk that he was Ms. Martin's representative and that she was waiting for him.

When Officer Teilhard introduced himself and shook Mack's hand, Mack cut through the Deep South niceties and said, "You're holding my client here. Hannah Martin."

Teilhard gave him a mocking look. "You're Ms. Martin's lawyer? Because I've got to say, you don't look like a lawyer."

"I'm an attorney," Mack said. "But I don't have a regular practice."

Teilhard's face began to take on a ruddy tint. "What the hell does that mean?"

"What are the charges against Ms. Martin?" Mack shot back.

Teilhard yawned. "Not sure yet. I haven't heard back from the prosecutor's office."

"But you know what you're holding her for."

The older detective laughed. "Yep. She is in a lot of trouble."

"And does she know why she's being held here?"

"Right now it's felony, grand theft of a vehicle."

Mack waited, but the detective didn't say anything else. "That's it?"

"For now," Teilhard said with a conspiratorial smile.

Mack had to bite his tongue to keep from asking about the drugs and Billy Joe Campbell's murder. He sure as hell didn't want to tip his hand. It had to be impossible that the detective didn't know both of those things. But Mack wasn't going to tell him.

When they stopped in front of the interrogation room, Mack put his hand on the knob, then paused. "Thanks," he said to Teilhard. "I want to speak to my client in confidence, please. No two-way mirror. No microphones. No recording. Can we do that?"

That earned him a laugh and a deceptively hard pat on the back. "Sure," he said. "Anything for Ms. Martin."

Mack decided he *really* didn't like Teilhard. "Thanks," he said sarcastically, then opened the door and went inside.

Hannah was sitting at an old, scratched, wooden table with a Formica top. She'd taken her hair out of its braid and was finger combing it over her right shoulder; her head was tilted to one side and her eyes were closed. To Mack, she looked like one of the beautiful, graceful and forlorn women Toulouse-Lautrec painted. *Woman Braiding Hair After Arrest.*

Not only did she appear forlorn, she also was even more bedraggled and exhausted than she'd been the morning before. He couldn't take his eyes off her. She was dressed in the same jeans and shirt. The shirt was even more wrinkled and had a small coffee stain on the front. Mack's heart wrenched when her face brightened at the sight of him.

"Hey, there, Hannah," he said. "You look like you slept in the holding tank last night." It was a feeble effort at coaxing a smile, but instead of responding in kind, her wide, sad eyes glimmered with tears. He pulled out a chair, glancing behind him at the mirror before he sat. It wasn't that he didn't trust Teilhard to honor his request for privacy, but there was always the chance that someone might accidentally leave the sound on.

Actually, it *was* that he didn't trust Teilhard.

"Are you okay? Do you need anything?" he asked.

Hannah closed her eyes and took a long breath. "Time travel, so I could go back and change a couple of things?"

To his dismay, he saw a tear leak out from beneath her closed eyelids. "How about some more coffee?" Before he finished the question, she was shaking her head.

"Ugh. No. Coffee you can see through is nothing but dirty water," she said distastefully. "Besides, I'm not sure I can keep anything down right now," she said. She stopped combing her hair with her fingers for a second to wipe her eye. "I'm so tired."

Mack reached into his pocket for a comb to offer her, but before he got his hands on it, she'd thrown her hair back over her shoulder and lifted her arms to braid it. Mack froze, unable to look away. The position of her arms caused her shirt to ride up above the low waistband of the jeans. The skin of her midriff and tummy was pale and smooth. While she was slender, she wasn't skinny. Her body was beautiful and sleek, with curves and muscles in all the right places.

What he wouldn't give to see her dressed like she ought to be—or undressed.

She looked up and caught him staring. To his surprise and chagrin, his face grew warm.

He quickly stood and paced, positioning himself out of her line of sight. What the hell? He'd seen women in all stages of dress and undress. He'd *been* in all stages of dress and undress in front of women. And he'd never blushed in his entire life.

He turned to look at the back of her head. Her fingers were entwined with her shiny, straw-colored hair. She twisted the strands back and forth and, as if by magic, they ended up as a fat, sleek braid. It was fascinating to watch, even though he couldn't keep up with her lightning-fast fingers. By the time she was more than halfway done and had pulled the hair over her shoulder to finish it, he found himself hoping that braid was easier to loosen than it was to braid. He hoped that pushing his fingers through the strands would cause them to unravel until they shimmered around her face and over her shoulders and slid through his fingers like liquid gold.

Then he grimaced and shook his head. He didn't like where his thoughts were headed. He'd already had a talk with himself about not allowing himself to think about her. It seemed that his subconscious mind had not paid attention. Otherwise why would all these thoughts be crowding his brain as soon as he laid eyes on her?

He'd come down here because she'd sounded so tired and so hopeless. That was all. He'd do what he had to in order to help her just enough so that she was able to get back to Dowdie, Texas. He wished he was hard-hearted enough to have refused to come, but that wasn't him. He'd help her. Then he'd forget her. He had to, for his own peace of mind.

He circled back around to his chair and sat down. "Have you been arraigned?" he asked.

She looked at him blankly for a brief moment. "I don't know. But I don't think so. That's in front of a judge, isn't it? They brought me in and questioned me for a long time. Then they locked me in a cell with two other women and left me there all night. Teilhard, the detective, wouldn't even let me make a phone call until this morning."

"What has Detective Teilhard been questioning you about?"

"Last night? He asked me all about the car and what happened to it. Then he wanted to know what happened to Billy Joe." She stopped. "Billy Joe Campbell is my mother's boyfriend."

He nodded. "What about this morning?"

She shook her head. "Nothing yet. He brought me in here but before he could say anything I told him I wanted my phone call. He said okay and left."

Mack rubbed his forehead, right at the hairline, where a small scar sometimes bothered him. So the detective hadn't brought up the connection between Billy Joe and the car and a suspected drug distribution ring operating in and around her hometown. Was that because he hadn't received official word from the prosecutor's office? "So what have you told him?"

"All I've done is answer his questions," she said, looking down at the desk.

"Oh, yeah?" he said, sending her an arch look. She didn't look up, so his expression was wasted. "Listen to me, Hannah. I get that you've got secrets you're not willing to tell. But if you want me to represent you, I've got to know what's going on with you."

She looked bewildered for a second. "Represent? What do you mean?"

"I mean represent. Remember I told you to tell them

you'd called your lawyer?" He gave her a small smile and spread his hands. "Here I am."

"You're a lawyer?" she said, staring at him, then she shook her head. "I don't want a lawyer. I didn't know you were one. I've got to get out of here. So I'm just going to let him arraign me for car theft. I can make bail and be out of here in a couple of hours."

Mack watched her face morph from bewildered and worried to satisfied and guileless. He had to wonder if she was that good, or if she really had no idea how much trouble she was in. "That's what you think? That you're going to waltz out of here in an hour or two with a slap on the wrist for stealing a car?"

She looked up at him, that furrow deepening between her brows.

"What about Billy Joe?"

She pressed her lips together for a second. "What about him?"

"Did Teilhard ask you about him?"

"He told me he was dead and asked me if I'd killed him." She paused. "But I told him I didn't."

"So who did? Did your mother?"

"What?" She looked genuinely stunned.

"You heard me. Did your mother kill Billy Joe Campbell?"

She shook her head. For a couple of seconds, Mack was sure that she was holding her breath. Then she pressed her fingers against her lips, then her palm, then her fist. Tears filled her eyes and spilled over to run down her face.

"What's wrong?"

She shook her head harder, then finally took a deep, gulping breath. "Nothing," she said, swiping at the wetness on her cheeks.

"You didn't answer my question."

"No," she whispered. "My mother didn't kill Billy Joe. But Billy Joe may have killed her."

"Because she needs dialysis," Mack said.

She nodded as more tears fell.

"But you know who did kill him, don't you?"

"No."

Mack studied her for a long time. She clasped her hands together in front of her and stared at them. Twice he saw tears fall onto the backs of her hands. "Are you lying, Hannah?" he asked.

She pressed her fingers against the bridge of her nose, then let out a long sigh. "No. I don't know. Not on purpose."

He leaned forward and placed his elbows on the table and clasped his hands. "Look at me."

She met his gaze, her red-rimmed, bloodshot eyes half-closed.

"You do know. And you are lying. You lied to me and now you're lying to the police, and I need to know why. Otherwise, how can I help you?"

She shook her head, her gaze not meeting his. "I'm not lying—"

Mack cut a hand through the air. "Yes, you are. Listen to me. You're in big trouble. Bigger than you may realize. Now, you've asked me for help. But I don't know a whit more about you or your problem than I did yesterday when you knocked on my door and then ran. Okay, I know a few things more, but that's all. *You* called *me*. But you're not telling me the truth. And as long as you lie to me, all I've got is whatever Teilhard digs up, and trust me when I tell you that I can't use that to help you." He shrugged. "Now one of the things I know is that you saw the man who shot Billy Joe, didn't you?"

She scraped her lower lip with her teeth. Her hands rubbed together nervously. She wouldn't meet his gaze.

Mack's stomach began to turn sour. "If you won't talk to me, I might as well leave, because there's nothing I can do for you. Listen, Hannah, I understand how afraid you are and I know how hard it is for you to trust anyone."

At that instant, the door opened and Teilhard came in, followed by a female officer.

Mack's anger flared. Another three seconds and he might have gotten her to talk. "What the hell? I asked for privacy," Mack demanded. "I'm not done. Not by a long shot."

"Sorry, Mr. Griffin," Teilhard said. "This is an urgent police matter."

Mack's sour stomach flipped upside down. This was it. It was what he'd tried to warn Hannah about. If she couldn't trust him, he couldn't help her.

"Hannah Martin, please stand," Teilhard went on, turning to face Hannah.

Mack scowled at the detective. "What's so all-fired important that you couldn't have waited a few minutes until I was done talking with her?" But Mack knew why Teilhard had barged in. He'd found the drugs. Reluctantly, he nodded at Hannah.

With a bewildered glance at him, she stood.

"Hannah Martin, you're under arrest for possession of Schedule II narcotics, trafficking in drugs and transporting drugs across state lines with the intent to sell."

Hannah swayed and probably would have fallen if the female officer hadn't taken her arm.

"Turn around," the officer said.

Teilhard smiled. "I guess you can see why this couldn't wait. One of our dogs went nuts when we walked him through the impound lot. Turns out the trunk of Ms. Martin's car, as well as some other strategic places, was lined with brand-new bottles of Oxycontin."

"Oxy—?" Hannah's face drained of color.

So she hadn't known about the drugs, or at least not for certain. Mack had seen some women who could lie without blinking an eye, but he'd never seen one who could turn white as a sheet on cue.

The policewoman recited the Miranda warning in a low monotone as Teilhard recounted to Mack all the minute details of the dog's excitement and the discovery of the drugs.

Mack watched Hannah as the policewoman cuffed her hands behind her back. She was still pale, and the desperation was back in her eyes. He knew that the ground he'd gained before Teilhard had burst in was gone. She was avoiding his gaze again. The doubt began to creep back into his mind.

"Mack?" Hannah said as the woman turned her back around.

Mack met her gaze and tried to send her a reassuring look, but in truth he wasn't sure he could get her out of this. He *knew* he should get himself out before he was in too deep. His need to get away from her had nothing to do with her guilt or innocence. That wasn't the issue here. Not for him.

His problem was his tendency to step in as rescuer and protector to any woman who seemed to need him. His own version of a knight in shining armor. He knew if he took Hannah's case, he'd work it until he won or she went to prison, and maybe even longer. And there was a very good chance that while working her case, he'd fall for her.

He supposed it was good that he understood his problem, even if he couldn't cure it. His need to play rescuer was one reason he'd quit his law practice, even though he'd always wanted to be a criminal attorney. He'd always seen himself as a champion against men who abused women. But it hadn't taken long for him to figure out that he wasn't cut out for the job. He was too quixotic to be effective in a courtroom. It required a level of dispassion he didn't possess to be a good defense attorney. He'd finally resigned his law practice and gotten a private investigator license, figuring he'd do better in a more hands-on role where he could put his passion to good use.

As soon as the policewoman was done reciting the Miranda warning, Mack cocked an eyebrow at Teilhard. "Hang on, Detective. You didn't follow the law in Ms. Martin's case. My client requested a telephone call and was not allowed one."

Teilhard's arrogant face froze. "Look, Griffin, she got her phone call. She called you, didn't she?"

"If she'd have been allowed that call last night, she wouldn't have had to spend the night in that holding cell. That was unnecessarily cruel."

"Cruel?" Teilhard laughed. "Are you soft on her or just soft in general? She's a felon. She didn't ask for a phone call last night as far as I know."

Mack let that drop. He'd made his point, and his first mistake. He should have said *punitive* instead of *cruel*. It was a more dispassionate term. Still, he'd given Teilhard notice. The SOB wouldn't get another chance to deny Hannah her rights.

"Well, *counselor,*" Teilhard went on. "Do you mind if I ask her a couple of questions?"

"Be my guest," Mack said, sending Hannah a reassuring look that he hoped she could read. "I'll sit right here."

Teilhard ignored him. "Ms. Martin, what were you planning to do with the drugs you transported from Texas into Louisiana?"

"I don't know anything about any drugs," Hannah said.

"You knew about them, all right. In fact, you drove here from Texas to deliver them, didn't you?"

When Hannah didn't answer right away, Teilhard leaned over the table. "Didn't you!" he shouted.

Mack started to intervene, but Hannah lifted her chin and answered. "No."

"But something happened, didn't it? Something that kept you from making that delivery. Did you run into your rivals? Is that how the rear bumper of your car got shot up?"

"I—can't answer that," she muttered, shaking her head. "I can't."

"It's not that you can't, is it?" Teilhard snapped, moving in for the kill. "It's that you—"

"Okay," Mack interrupted, sick of Teilhard's bullying. "That's enough. I don't think you have a case at all, Detective. You have no connection between Ms. Martin and the drugs found in the car." Mack was flying blind now. But he figured his version of what Hannah had done was as plausible as the detective's. "She took the vehicle in question because it was the only working vehicle to which she had access."

Teilhard rolled his eyes. "Tell it to the judge," he said.

"I need some time with my client," Mack said coldly.

Chapter Six

Hannah watched Mack and Detective Teilhard as they faced off, arguing about her rights. She'd been stunned when Mack said he was representing her. So now he was not just a private investigator. He was an *attorney*.

For Hannah, attorneys were another of those authorities whose job had seemed to be to threaten her mother and her. It was the lawyers who set things in motion to take children away from their parents.

But Mack didn't look like any lawyer she ever remembered seeing. Rabb, the lawyer handling her mother's estate, wore baggy suits and looked as though he'd just eaten something sour. The lawyers she remembered from her childhood were always tightly done up in their stiff suits and their striped ties. They all had the same sour expression as Rabb, but her memory of them was of giants towering over her and patting her on the head. And even as a little girl, she'd known that they held infinite power over her in their gnarly hands.

But Mack was dressed in crisply pressed pants and a yellow shirt with the sleeves rolled up. No tie and no coat. He leaned against the wall, one leg casually crossed over the other. He could have been standing at a water cooler discussing last night's scores, his body language was that relaxed.

But not his face. His face wasn't casual or relaxed. But it wasn't sour, either. From the businesslike haircut to the high, sculpted cheekbones to his straight nose and wide mouth all the way down to the small cleft in his chin, Mack's face was a study in control. She didn't miss the slight flexing of the muscle in his jaw or the shadow in his hazel eyes when he glanced in her direction.

She couldn't understand why he was even here. She'd called him because she was desperate and his was the only phone number she had. But she hadn't expected him to come. After all, why would he, a complete stranger, bother with her?

From the first moment she'd seen him, she'd been attracted to him. And she knew he'd been interested in her. That had been obvious from the glint in his eyes as they roamed down and back up her body. But as soon as she'd mentioned his mother's name, he'd withdrawn.

She didn't know what he and Teilhard were arguing about, but she got the dynamic. Whatever it was, the point was to establish the playing field. It was a jockeying for position and a struggle to see who was top dog. An arrow of apprehension lodged in her heart. She'd had enough of arrogant, bullying men who couldn't believe a woman could think for herself. Was Mack one of those? She hadn't thought so, but every so often, he glanced in her direction, his eyes hard and his mouth tight-lipped and disapproving. If there was one thing she knew, it was that Mack Griffin disapproved of her. So why was he here?

Detective Teilhard's cell phone rang, interrupting the two men. Teilhard answered in the middle of something Mack was saying. Hannah saw Mack's jaw flex.

"Detective Teilhard," he said, then listened. "Yeah,

sure." He hung up the phone, sent Mack a glance that could only be described as triumphant and turned to the female officer who stood by the door.

"Get her ready for arraignment, Officer Jeraux," Teilhard said.

"Who was that?" Mack asked. "The D.A.'s office?"

"Wow. Got it in one. You *must* be a lawyer," Teilhard mocked. "They're charging Ms. Martin with grand theft auto, transporting Schedule II narcotics across state lines, possession of a felony amount of narcotics for purposes of transporting across state lines and possession of Schedule II narcotics for the purpose of distribution or sale."

Hannah listened, holding her breath, as Teilhard spewed out the awful, frightening charges. But when he finished, there was one charge missing. Murder. Why were they not charging her with Billy Joe Campbell's murder? And why had no one mentioned her mother? Surely Teilhard had to have talked to Sheriff Harlan King in Dowdie. What if her mother had been found? What if they'd charged her sick mother with Billy Joe's murder?

Suddenly, she felt light-headed and sick to her stomach. She didn't realize that her legs had collapsed until a pair of lean, strong arms caught her and guided her to a chair as if she was weightless. When her eyes fluttered open, she found herself looking into Mack Griffin's greenish-gold ones.

He said something, but there was a loud roaring in her ears, so all she knew was that he was frowning at her and his lips were moving.

"Wha—?" She was trying to say "What?" but all that came out was a small groan.

"—did she last eat?" she heard Mack say over the

roaring in her ears. It was a good question. She certainly didn't remember. The only thing she'd had all night was a couple of swallows of water from the fountain in the cell.

"I don't have time for this, Griffin. We're due in court in fifteen minutes."

"And as soon as we walk in, I'll ask the judge for a delay and accuse you of police brutality and violating Ms. Martin's rights."

Hannah stared at Mack in surprise. He might not look like a lawyer, but he certainly sounded like one.

"Now please get her something to eat."

Teilhard sighed. "Jeraux, get her a sandwich and a Coke, would you?"

The thought of a limp, stale sandwich from a vending machine turned Hannah's stomach, but a Coke sounded good. She hoped it would soothe the burning fear inside her. The fear that she would go to prison and her mother would die.

Just as she'd thought, Hannah couldn't swallow a bite of the droopy ham sandwich, but the Coke—or more specifically its sugar and caffeine—bolstered her energy a little. It didn't erase the fact that she hadn't slept more than a couple of hours the night before, but it did seem to wash away some of the haze from her brain and make her feel a little less like she were carrying around a hundred-pound lead weight. It settled her stomach a little, too.

She was led into the courtroom by a female officer and shown where to sit. She couldn't believe how relieved she was when she saw Mack sitting there waiting for her.

"Mack," she whispered, putting her hand on his arm. She wanted to ask him why Billy Joe's murder hadn't come up in the list of charges levied against her. But he eyed her hand with a frown and shook his head.

"I need to know—" she started, but at that instant, the bailiff appeared in the front of the courtroom and shouted, "All rise. Now entering the courtroom is the Honorable Vivien Gold."

There was a muffled rustle of clothes, a number of sighs and a few grunts as everyone in the courtroom got to their feet. She stood with them and glanced sidelong at Mack, who was studying the judge. From his broad, straight shoulders to the cuffs of his neatly pressed slacks, he was every inch the successful young attorney, one of the authority figures that Hannah had been taught to avoid at all costs. She had seen and talked to him for barely more than one hour, yet of all the people she'd known in her life, including her mother, he was the most stable, the most dependable and, she had a feeling, the strongest.

And she regretted ever knocking on his door or using her one phone call to call him. The trouble with Mack was that she could easily learn to depend on him, and that could not happen. Ever! After watching her alcoholic mother get into one train wreck of a relationship after another, Hannah had vowed that she would never be dependent on another person.

The only person she could trust was herself. Everyone else in her life had proved to be untrustworthy. She might be in for a lonely life, but at least she would be in control of her own destiny, and she'd never be betrayed or abandoned or— She tried to stop the thought, but her brain was already all over it.

Or loved. Still, wasn't that a small price to pay to avoid being hurt? She nodded to herself. Yes. It was.

The sharp, startling rap of wood against wood reminded her that she was *not* in control of her own destiny yet. She was subject to the whim of a stern woman in black robes. As the Honorable Vivien Gold pounded the gavel one last time and frowned at the courtroom, Hannah tried to see behind the severe expression down to the woman beneath.

Judge Gold called the first case up for arraignment. Mack stood and nodded at Hannah, then stepped into the center aisle as the bailiff read her name and the charges against her. The policewoman nudged her. "Stand up," she whispered.

Hannah did.

"How does the defendant plead?" Judge Gold asked, peering over her reading glasses.

Mack glanced at her and inclined his head toward the judge.

"Well?" the judge prodded.

"Not guilty," Mack prompted quietly.

"Not guilty," she said, her voice a raspy whisper.

"Speak up, Ms.—" Judge Gold glanced down at a sheet of paper "—Martin."

"Yes, ma'am," Hannah said, more steadily. "Not guilty."

The judge repeated the charges aloud, then looked up at Hannah. The courtroom was silent and Hannah did her best not to squirm while the judge examined her for a long moment, then looked back at the charges. Finally, she addressed Mack.

"Mr. Griffin, I'm inclined to remand your client until trial, given the nature of the charges against her."

"Your Honor," Mack said, "Ms. Martin knows nothing about any drugs, nor did she know that the vehicle that she borrowed was stolen."

"Your Honor," the prosecutor said. "Mr. Griffin's

statement could be correct. But the defendant has continually refused to answer any questions about why she drove to south Louisiana. She also refuses to answer any questions about her mother's whereabouts. And that, Your Honor, is exactly why she should be remanded. Her mother is a resident in Dowdie, Texas, but she currently seems to be missing. Therefore, there is nothing to keep Ms. Martin here. And then there is the severity of the crimes and the quantity of the drugs found in her possession."

"Objection, Your Honor," Mack said. "The drugs were not in her possession. They were well hidden in a vehicle she *borrowed*."

"Your Honor—" the prosecutor protested, standing.

The gavel rapped again. "Yes, yes, yes, Mr. Simpson," she said to the prosecutor. Then she waved a hand in Mack's direction. "Mr. Griffin, this is an arraignment. You have no right to objection. We merely need a plea, which we have, and a decision on bail, which we are about to have. But first, I want to ask Ms. Martin a few questions."

Hannah looked up, surprised.

"Ms. Martin," Judge Gold said kindly, "where does your mother live?"

"In Dowdie, Texas, Your Honor," she replied, swallowing against a lump that grew in her throat. She was determined not to break down.

"And how is she?"

"She's not well, Your Honor. She has liver disease."

"I'm sorry to hear that. Do you understand that you are being arraigned on some very serious charges and that if you are let out on bail, you may not leave this jurisdiction?"

"Y-yes, Your Honor."

The judge leaned back in her chair again. "Mr. Griffin, Mr. Simpson, I'll hear one more sentence—one sentence—from each of you, but I must tell you, Mr. Griffin, I'm inclined to remand."

Hannah felt her eyes stinging. She was going to have to go back to jail, back to that cold, harsh place, for who knew how long. Terror nearly sheared the air from her lungs. She bit her lip, hard, and concentrated on holding back tears.

"Your Honor, if I may." Mack spoke quickly. "I request that Ms. Martin be released on my recognizance. I will post bail as well, as assurance that Ms. Martin does not leave the jurisdiction."

Hannah gaped at him. "What are you doing?" she whispered, grabbing the sleeve of his jacket.

"Your Honor, I object!" the prosecutor cried.

The gavel rapped. "Quiet, everyone. Mr. Simpson, I shouldn't have to explain again that this is not the place for objections," she said to the prosecutor, then turned to Mack. "Mr. Griffin? You understand the responsibility you're undertaking?"

"Yes, Your Honor, I do."

"Ms. Martin, is this acceptable to you?"

Hannah didn't have a clue what was going on. It sounded to her like Mack was proposing something similar to posting bail for her. She gave a mental shake of her head. Mack Griffin had no idea of the mess he was getting into by taking responsibility for her. She looked at his big, capable hands, his broad shoulders, the taut, determined line of his jaw.

With regret, because by the time all this was over, he was going to hate her for getting him mixed up in her life, she nodded reluctantly. "Yes, Your Honor," she murmured.

"Speak up, Ms. Martin."

"Yes, Your Honor. It's acceptable." She felt her throat close on the word *acceptable*.

The gavel hitting the wooden block rang through the courtroom again and Judge Gold called out, "Thank you." Then she nodded at the bailiff, who stepped forward. "You are dismissed," he said to them. Then he took a breath and spoke loudly. "Next case."

BACK AT THE police station an officer put Hannah and Mack in a cubicle and gave them a stack of forms to sign. Hannah tried to ask Mack what all the forms were for, but she never got the chance because the officer was rushing her through them so fast. Neither Mack nor any of the other officers seemed to be worried about that. Once all the forms were signed, Hannah was told she could leave, as long as she left with Mack. So they walked outside together.

As Hannah stepped outside, she squinted in the noonday sun like a newly released convict. The heat on her head and face caused her to yawn drowsily. She'd never understood the expression bone tired until that moment.

With a sigh, she turned and held out her hand to Mack. "Thank you for posting bail for me. I'll pay you back someday. My mother was right, sending me to Kathleen Griffin's house. I don't know what I'd have done without you. Please bill me for your time."

He frowned at her. "Hang on a minute," he said. "Do you not know what *recognizance* is?"

She sighed and shook her head. "I'm going to guess it's some sort of legal responsibility. I'm responsible for coming back to court when they call me." She held up a hand. "And I'm sure it's expensive, but I promise I'll pay you back. I hope to have part of the payment when I come back here for the first trial date."

"Not a bad definition," he said. "But wrong. It's actually an obligation of record entered into before a court, with a condition to do some act required by law. That act is therein specified. In this case, *I'm* the one who agreed to do the act, said act being take full responsibility for your actions, including keeping you within the law and within the conditions of the recognizance."

Hannah didn't understand most of what he'd said. The words floated past her like dandelion puffs on a breeze, their meaning as scattered as the flower's airborne seeds in the exhausted haze that enveloped her brain.

"In short, you're my responsibility," Mack went on. "So, no. You will not slip out of here like a fox and go back to Texas. You're staying with me. And you're going to explain to me just what's going on with you."

"Nothing's going on with me." She held up a hand. "Look, Mr. Griffin. All I want to do is get back to Dowdie. My mother is there. She's—sick. I've got to take care of her. I'm not going anywhere else." She dug in her purse for her phone and searched for taxicabs.

"What are you doing?" he asked, trying to see the phone's display.

"Looking for a taxi service. I need to get back to my motel."

"Did you hear me?" he said. "You're coming with me."

She used her thumb to flip pages on the phone. "No, I'm not," she said without looking up. "You're not responsible for me. I have to get some sleep."

"Sorry, sweetheart. Lawyer trumps sleepy client. Now, my car is right over there." He held out his hand.

"No," she said, stepping backward. "I'm not going with you. I can't. I have to get back to Dowdie. In case you've forgotten, my mother is missing."

He frowned. "I know, Hannah. And I understand how badly you want to get back there, but Judge Gold issued a court order that says you have to stay here. Now, don't worry. You can tell me everything when we get to the house and—"

"I said *no!*" Hannah was so tired she wanted to cry, but she was so tired of crying. Her eyes burned. Her cheeks stung where the tears had chapped them. And it made her vulnerable, exactly like depending on another person did. Sure, it sounded easy to let Mack take care of her. She knew he could and would. She could tell that just by looking at him.

But during all those hours as she'd driven east from Dowdie, Texas, with no idea where she was going or what she would do once she got there, she'd renewed a vow she'd made years before, when her mother had gotten sick.

Nobody, *nobody,* would control Hannah Martin's life except Hannah Martin. Billy Joe had tried to control her the same way he'd controlled her mother and she'd let him, because she'd hoped he could make her mother happy, but he'd turned out to be a piece of scum, just like most of her other boyfriends. But even if her mother couldn't learn from her mistakes, Hannah could. She'd renewed her vow and she would never break it again.

She realized she was shaking her head and Mack was staring at her.

"Okay," he said, shrugging. "Let's go back inside. I'll need to call the prosecutor and get some paperwork filled out."

"More paperwork?" she sighed. "I can't believe

there's anything we didn't already fill out and sign. Can't you just call me a cab?"

"If you're firing me as your attorney, then yeah. There's going to be a lot more paperwork. And no, I can't just call you a cab. Hannah," he said, "look at me."

She lifted her drooping eyelids to meet his gaze.

"You'll have to go before another judge. This time you *will* be remanded. They'll put you back in jail."

She didn't even bother to answer. He'd defeated her. He knew she wouldn't go back in there. She sighed in exasperation. She was stuck with Mack. Oh, she knew he could keep her safe. She'd known that from the first instant she'd seen him. She also knew she could fight her attraction to him. She didn't have time for that kind of nonsense.

But everything came at a price. Mack's price for taking care of her would be her secrets. He'd want to know everything, and she'd never told *anyone* everything. So why would she tell him?

Chapter Seven

"My car is right there," Mack said.

She followed the nod of his head and saw a large, black Jaguar parked next to an old white BMW 3-series. "The Jag, right?"

It surprised her when he bypassed the Jag to unlock the BMW. She'd have bet money on him being a Jaguar guy. Especially since he was at least six feet two inches tall and the Jag seemed so much larger than the Beemer.

Plus, she'd never ridden in a Jag. Of course, she'd never ridden in a BMW, either. When she got in on the passenger's side, she sank down into a contoured leather seat that felt as though it had been made just for her. To her relief, the car was quiet and elegantly smooth.

As Mack pulled out into traffic, she sank more deeply into the seat, closed her eyes and shaded them from the brightness with her hand. The next thing she knew, Mack's warm hand was on her arm and he was quietly saying her name.

She didn't want to open her eyes, didn't want to be pulled away from the soft, dark haze of sleep back into bright, burning reality. "What?" she muttered irritably.

"We're home. You need to wake up."

The words, delivered in a deep, intriguing rumble,

roused her a bit. She forced one eye open. "Home?" Had he really said *home?*

He opened the driver's-side door. "Come on."

"Mmm," she mumbled without moving. The driver's-side door slammed and there was nothing but peaceful silence. Then the passenger door opened and she nearly tumbled out, saved only by her seat belt and Mack's hand catching her arm.

Not willing to wake up completely, she fumbled with the belt until Mack reached across her to release the belt with the deftness of a magician. When he leaned in close, a subtle scent wafted past her nostrils. She couldn't identify it but it was nice. It was Mack.

"Let's go," he said. "I want to get you up the stairs and into bed before you fall so fast asleep that I can't move you."

He guided her up the front porch steps and through the front door.

"Do you want a soda and a sandwich? I just bought some fresh deli."

The idea of anything in her stomach made her feel queasy. She shook her head as she set her purse down on the kitchen counter. "Just water, please."

He filled a glass from the refrigerator-door water dispenser and handed it to her. She drank gratefully. The water felt cool going down and she knew exactly when it hit her empty stomach. "Where's the bedroom?" she asked hopefully.

"Hannah. We need to talk—just for a few minutes. Teilhard interrupted us before you told me about Billy Joe Campbell's murder. Right now all I know is that he was shot and you saw it and took off in his car. I believe the police know a lot more than that and I *know* you do."

Hannah didn't want to talk about Billy Joe anymore.

What she wanted to do was figure out a way to get back to Dowdie and find her mother. What she had to do first was sleep. "Why are you doing all this?" she asked.

"All what?" he responded, looking puzzled and defensive.

"Helping me. Being my lawyer. Why are you going to all this trouble for a stranger?"

"You're not a stranger," he said, avoiding her gaze. "Your mom and mine were best friends. You came here looking for her to help you and what you got was me."

"But you didn't want to help. You didn't want to have anything to do with me." He still wasn't looking at her. She frowned. "What changed your mind?"

"You called me from the police station. You—needed my help." He gave a little shrug, as if that covered everything.

Something in his voice meshed with something her subconscious mind had been trying to figure out ever since they first met. "But that's just it. I got the definite impression that you don't like being needed."

Mack's gaze darkened for an instant, then he looked away. He gave a short chuckle. "That doesn't make sense. I'm a private investigator. My whole job depends on people needing me."

"No," Hannah said thoughtfully. "Your clients don't need *you*. They need your services."

"Same thing."

"No, it's not." She was much too sleepy to figure out where she was going with that thought, but she knew she was right. Mack had not wanted to help her. So why had he?

"You came to my mother's home seeking help. I didn't help you. If I had, you might not have had to spend the night in the tank. I feel like I let you down. I feel responsible for you."

"Well, trust me, you're not. I can take care of myself, believe me. I've been doing it all my life. I appreciate you coming down there and getting me out of jail…" Hannah interrupted herself by yawning. She rubbed her eyes. "But I've got to get back to Dowdie. My mother can't—" Her breath caught. "She can't last much longer."

Mack nodded solemnly. "I know. But you can't do anything until you've had some rest. You sure can't take off for Dowdie on your own."

"Of course I can. I got here on my own."

"Hannah, you need to think about your situation," Mack said. "First, there was about two hundred thousand dollars' worth of drugs in that car you were driving. The car and the drugs have been impounded and placed into evidence by the police. Do you know anyone by the name Ficone?"

Hannah closed her eyes and shook her head. *Ficone.* She'd heard the name before, but where? She was trying to think, trying to listen to what Mack was saying, but between the sleepy haze in her brain and a growing queasiness in her stomach, she was finding it very hard to concentrate.

"Sal Ficone is a crime boss who operates out of Galveston," Mack said. "He's a very dangerous man in a very dangerous business. If those were his drugs, he's going to be looking for you."

"Looking for me?" she echoed, not quite able to make sense of what Mack was saying. She rubbed her temple, then took a small sip of water, hoping it would stop the queasiness. She knew she needed to eat, but she needed sleep even more.

"That's right. And depending on what's happening with the Dowdie sheriff's investigation of your mother's boyfriend's murder, you may be facing murder or manslaughter charges."

"You think I killed him?" she asked sharply.

Mack pushed his fingers through his hair and sighed. "That's the problem, Hannah. I have no idea."

Hannah put her hands over her face and groaned. "I can't take this. I'm so sleepy I can't think, and I feel sick. I don't care about Billy Joe right now. I just need to sleep for a couple of hours and then get home and find my mom."

Mack didn't say anything. Hannah spread her fingers and peered through them at Mack. His gaze was steady and neutral and for some reason that made her angry.

"I—didn't—kill—him," she said through clenched teeth. She crossed her arms, hugging herself. "When I got back from buying beer for Billy Joe, I heard yelling from the garage. I went out there and peeked in the side door. I saw a big man in a dark T-shirt with a red tattoo on the back of his wrist, holding a gun on Billy Joe. He was accusing Billy Joe of stealing from his boss." She stopped. "Ficone," she said. "I think the man did call his boss Mr. Ficone."

Mack's brows rose and his expression turned grim. "If Billy Joe was stealing from Sal Ficone, I'm surprised he lasted as long as he did. Go on."

"I couldn't believe it. Billy Joe was blubbering, trying to get the guy to put the gun away. Then he threw me under the bus, the coward. The man was accusing Billy Joe of stealing money and drugs from Ficone. Anyhow, Billy Joe told him I was the one who'd stolen the stuff. The man seemed disgusted that Billy Joe would try to blame someone else. But Billy Joe kept telling him that I took the money. That I was the key. The man called him a liar and Billy Joe pulled a gun." She stopped, out of breath because the memory squeezed her chest tight.

"And the man just shot him. Right in the middle of his chest. Blood went everywhere. And his back—the back of his shirt—all of a sudden it blossomed with blood. Billy Joe just fell." Her voice broke. "Now he's dead and he's the only one in the world who knew where my mom is."

"Did the man see you?" Mack asked.

She nodded. "He looked at me—" She stopped. "He shot at me. I don't know why he didn't hit me." She closed her eyes. "I think I turned a ladder over in front of the door."

"I'm not sure how you didn't get shot, either. But I suspect it's because they need you. How did you manage to get away? It sounds like the killer knew the drugs were in the Toyota."

She set the cold glass down on the counter and clasped her hands. "All I could do was run. He was behind me, shooting. I thought I was dead. Then I realized I still had Billy Joe's keys in my hand. So I jumped in the car and took off. All I could think about was that a bullet was going to hit me before I could get into the car and drive away. I don't think I've ever been so scared."

Mack gazed at her, his hazel eyes clouded. "So you drove off in a car that you knew was full of drugs?"

"I was running for my life."

Mack nodded. "If you hadn't, you'd probably be dead, too. It sounds like Billy Joe died before he hit the floor."

Mack's words brought the sight of Billy Joe's blood rushing back to her.

"I think there was so much blood so fast, because the bullet hit his heart."

"I didn't think about that," she said. "The blood just—" She tried to demonstrate by spreading the fingers of both hands to simulate a flower opening, but stopped as an overwhelming nausea began to churn in her stomach. She swallowed acrid saliva. "Oh," she gasped, putting a hand over her mouth.

"What's the matter?" Mack asked.

"I'm— Where's the—bathroom?"

Thank goodness Mack didn't waste any time. He grabbed her arm and guided her quickly to the bathroom. She knelt in front of the toilet just in time. Her stomach heaved, but there was almost nothing in it to come up.

After a moment the spasms eased. She coughed a few times against the acid that burned in her throat, then started to push herself to her feet. To her surprise, Mack's warm hands helped her up and he gave her a cool, wet washcloth. Thankfully, she buried her face in it, breathing the air that was cooled by the damp cloth and letting its coolness take away the last dregs of queasiness.

When she raised her head, she felt dizzy. She grabbed at the edge of the sink, but Mack was watching her closely and caught her. He pulled her close. "Are you going to faint on me again?" he asked with a smile.

"No," she said. "At least I don't think so." She closed her eyes and, just for a moment, let herself be held by him. It was dangerous; it could leave her with a longing and an emptiness that she might never fill, if she got too used to it. But she didn't plan to be around him long enough to get used to it.

Finally, she pushed away, merely leaving one hand

resting on his arm as she tried to stand alone. She waited, wondering if the nausea was going to come back.

"Want to sit for a minute?" he asked, putting the toilet seat cover down.

"No. Can you wait—outside?" she asked, mortified that she'd thrown up in front of him. Even more mortified that her face was sweaty, her eyes were tearing and her breath was undoubtedly awful.

"Sure, if you think you're okay. I don't want you to fall."

"Please," she begged, gripping the edges of the sink like a lifeline.

He frowned at her for a moment, then stepped out of the bathroom and closed the door behind him.

Hannah sluiced her face with cold water for a long time, until her skin was no longer hot. Then she cupped her hands and rinsed her mouth. After carefully swallowing a mouthful or two of water to test her stomach, she looked around for mouthwash. She found some in the cabinet below the sink.

Before she could go back to the bedroom, she had to sit on the closed toilet seat for a moment, until a wave of light-headedness passed. Finally, she opened the door. Mack was waiting right outside.

"Better?" he asked.

"I need to lie down in bed," she said hoarsely.

"Sure," he said as he assessed her. "You're still pale."

"At least I'm not nauseated anymore."

He helped her from the bathroom into the bedroom. When she saw the double bed, Hannah uttered a half moan, half sigh.

Mack's hand touched the small of her back. "Are you going to be sick again?" he asked.

She shook her head, almost ready to cry at the sight of the soft, comfortable-looking bed. "It's a bed," she said, her gaze soothed by the sight of the tan bedspread and a brown afghan folded across the foot.

Mack laughed. "You sound like you haven't seen a bed in months."

"That's how I feel," she replied. "Is this your bedroom?"

"Nope. Mine's across the hall."

Hannah reached for the bedspread to fold it back, but Mack said, "Hannah? I need to get the key to your motel room before you go to sleep."

She sat down on the bed. "Key?" she echoed, then coughed and winced. Her throat was raw from throwing up.

He touched her cheek as if he was brushing an eyelash away. "I know you're sick and exhausted, but I need you to pay attention for a minute. Give me your key card so I can go fetch your stuff. Where's your purse?"

"Kitchen?" she said, ending it as a question, because her exhausted, queasy brain couldn't remember for sure. "Inside pocket, I think. But there's nothing at the motel. Mama always said keep everything important in…purse." She lay down.

She was almost asleep when his voice roused her.

"Never heard of The Metairie Haven Motel."

"Says a lot for your morals," Hannah said, yawning. "And taste." She closed her eyes and let herself relax down into the soft warmth of the bedclothes. She wasn't sure she'd ever felt anything so wonderful.

Several seconds later, she heard a clink near her head. Mack had brought her a glass of water. Then she felt him slipping off her shoes. His hands were warm against her cool skin.

"Hannah?" he said softly. "I'll be back within the hour. I'll lock the door behind me. You try to sleep."

"Good plan," she said. She sighed and stretched, willing every part of her body to relax. There were no words for how good the soft bed felt. Closing her eyes, she tried to wipe her mind clean of all the questions, all the worry, all the fear, and sink into blessed dreamless sleep. A deliciously soft warmth spread over her. It was Mack again, covering her with the bedspread.

"Sleep tight," he said softly, brushing his fingers across her chin. Then she felt something wonderful and warm on her cheek. Mack Griffin kissed her.

That kiss made her feel safer and more sheltered than she'd ever felt in her life. He would keep her safe.

MACK WATCHED HANNAH for a few moments as she slept, just to be sure she was okay, he told himself. But inside his head, his brain was screaming, *What was that all about?* Why had he kissed her? It was only a peck, meant to comfort her. In the short time he'd known her, he'd seen her wary, afraid, angry and pensive, but this was the first time she'd been relaxed and at ease.

Her eyes were softly closed. Her bare eyelids appeared blue from the veins that showed through the nearly translucent skin. Her lips were slightly parted and her breaths were barely audible, even and deep. She was asleep.

After a few seconds, he realized he was staring at her lips. He straightened and arched his neck, then checked his watch. He needed to leave so he could get back before rush-hour traffic. He'd wanted to go by the motel and see what, if anything, she'd left there, but she'd been so exhausted, he'd hated to delay getting her into bed.

That was probably a very good idea, considering that she'd gotten so sick.

She'd be safe in here. He had double-locking dead bolts, ensuring that nobody could get in. She hadn't slept in two days, so he doubted she would stir for hours.

As if to prove him wrong, her breath hitched and she shifted her legs beneath the afghan.

His gaze followed her movements. Her body was barely outlined under the light cover, trim and fit. But as he'd noticed before, she was not fashion-model skinny, like his usual dates. Nothing about Hannah fit his preferences in women. He knew himself and he knew his type and she was not it. He leaned toward tall, lean and leggy. Hannah was small and curvy. She was everything that he didn't want in a woman, not just physically but emotionally, too, everything that made him wary. But it all added up to the most fascinating woman he'd ever met. And the most dangerous.

He forced his gaze away from her before interest grew into desire and desire grew into arousal. He needed to get her key card and get going.

Her purse was on the kitchen counter. Reaching inside, he encountered a leather wallet, a small zippered bag that probably contained personal items, a pen, a small pad, the large, heavy key ring that must have held twenty keys and an envelope. He pulled out the envelope, his ears tuned toward the bedroom in case Hannah decided to get up.

The writing on its front was familiar. He'd just seen it on the back of the photo Hannah had showed him. It was her mother's. Stephanie Clemens.

She had written, *To My Daughter, Hannah Claire Martin.* Then in a different color ink—*To Be Opened in the Event of Stephanie Clemens's Death.*

Mack's heart twisted. He wondered why Hannah had the letter now, if her mother was still alive. He turned it over to look at the seal. It was self-sealing and ridiculously easy to open. Retrieving a small magnifying glass from a drawer, he examined the flap more closely. It was pristine, no wrinkles or tears. She hadn't opened it. He took out his pocketknife and carefully pried the flap up.

With a crooked smile, Mack pulled out the letter. He wasn't even pretending that there might be something in the letter that could help him with Hannah's legal case. He just wanted to know more about her.

He glanced toward the bedroom as he took out the letter and unfolded it.

My Darling Hannah, he read.

I've never told you anything about your family. I always told myself that it was for your own good. I think I wanted to believe that, but of course that's not true.

Mack skimmed the intimate words, looking for anything that would tell him anything about Hannah or the people she'd gotten herself mixed up with. But it was a very personal letter between mother and daughter, and as he read on, he felt guiltier and guiltier about invading Hannah's privacy.

Then, toward the bottom of the handwritten page, he saw something that stunned him to his core.

Your grandmother is Claire Delancey. She is the sister of Robert Connor Delancey—

Mack stopped. He blinked and read the words again, but they hadn't changed. *Your grandmother is Claire Delancey.* "Holy—" he whispered.

He turned and looked toward his guest bedroom again, feeling an urge to go back in there. He wanted to study Hannah's face in the light of this new knowledge, to see if he could see any resemblance. *Delancey.* Hannah was a Delancey. *Whoa.*

Or was she? Was all this an elaborate scam to get money from the Delanceys? It was pretty hard to believe that Hannah's mother happened to be best friends with Mack's mother and Mack worked for Dawson Delancey. But it was even harder to believe that Hannah was that deceitful—with her pale skin and its tendency to flush or drain of color at the slightest provocation.

Mack skimmed the rest of the letter, torn between believing and doubting. He needed to call Dawson and ask him about his aunt and whether she'd ever had a child. But not now. He reinserted the letter into the envelope and pressed the flap down. Good as new. He stuck the envelope back in Hannah's purse.

Then he dug deeper and found her phone. He'd been impressed that Detective Teilhard had let her have it. These days, cell phone service providers provided the police with CDs and transcripts of voice mail and texts, as well as address listings and anything else recorded on the SIM card of the phone. There was seldom any reason for them to hold on to the physical phone. For a minute, he studied the phone, familiarizing himself with its functions, reviewing the few names in her address book and recording his phone number in her phone and entering hers into his. Finally, he went to her voice mail. When prompted for the pass code, he tried the default, which was the last four digits of her phone number. It worked.

He retrieved the messages. The first one was from a Steve Rabb asking her to come to his office to sign the papers appointing her as her mother's power of attorney.

Rabb was obviously a lawyer, and his tone told Mack

that he felt as though Hannah's paltry legal needs were beneath him.

The next message showed the caller I.D. as B.J. That had to be Billy Joe Campbell. Mack pressed the play button. What spewed out was an angry tirade, punctuated by curses and epithets. Billy Joe called Hannah a bitch and shrieked at her for driving his *bleeping* car after he'd told her not to touch the *bleeping* thing. Then he told her that she'd better be home with his beer within ten minutes or her mother would *bleeping* pay for every minute she was late.

By the time the message was over, Mack's hand was shaking with anger. The guy was probably lucky that he was dead. Saved Mack the trouble of killing him or at the least beating him within an inch of his worthless life. He listened as the third message played.

Where'd you go, Hannah? I know you don't want to talk to me, but I need to see you, talk to you. I need to make sure you're all right. Call me as soon as possible and let me know where you are. I'm worried about you. Bye-bye, Hannah.

The electronic voice told him that was the last message and gave him a choice of options. He pressed Replay and listened to the last message again. There was something odd about the caller's voice. His tone and his words didn't go together. The words could be interpreted as concerned and friendly, but the voice was creepy, low in tone and volume, yet menacing.

Mack moved on to the skipped and erased messages. There was nothing there but an earlier tirade by Campbell. Was that it? Four messages? Two from Billy Joe, one from the attorney and one from the creep, whomever he was.

To be thorough, Mack checked everything a second

time and saw a tiny icon on the settings menu that he hadn't noticed the first time around. When he touched it, the words *voice memo* came up. He pressed the button, expecting to find nothing. But there was one recording.

He played it and heard the same menacing voice as in the voice mail message he'd just listened to.

Hannah had hit the record button. Smart.

Mack listened to the man trying to get Hannah to tell him where she was and to meet him. He kept insisting that Billy Joe had given her something. She kept insisting that he hadn't.

Hannah's voice sounded terrified as she said, "I don't know who you are and I don't have anything. Billy Joe didn't give me anything. Leave me alone!" The man insisted that Billy Joe had said she was the key, which meant she knew where Billy Joe had hidden everything.

Then the man said, "Oh, by the way, your mom says hi."

Mack heard Hannah's gasp. "Wait! You know where my mother is—?"

Mack heard an odd, short laugh, then there was a click and a dead sound on the line.

"Wait—please. No, no, no."

Mack knew it was the same voice. The low, menacing one. But Mack was focusing on the last thing he'd said before he'd said goodbye and how much it had obviously hurt Hannah, judging by the brokenhearted tone of her voice.

He'd said, "by the way, your mom says hi." The words sent a chill down Mack's spine. No wonder Hannah was desperate. But it was Billy Joe who'd abducted her mother. How would this man have found out where the woman was?

Mack played the recorded conversation a second time and was more chilled by the man's tone and words than he had been the first time he'd heard it. He thought about letting Teilhard know about the recording, but he wasn't sure the detective would appreciate it or use it if Mack was the one who gave it to him.

Once he was in his car and on his way to Metairie, Mack called Dawson. He wished he'd been able to bring the letter with him, but he hadn't dared. If Hannah had woken up and found the letter gone, he'd be in big trouble trying to explain why.

Dawson's phone rang until it went to voice mail.

"Dawson," Mack said. "I need to ask you something and it can't wait until y'all get back. Call me on my cell as soon as you pick up this message." He hung up, then thought about his message. Should he have left Dawson more information, maybe told him about the letter?

No. He wanted to talk to Dawson, not leave a cryptic message. Part of the reason he didn't want to put that information in a message was that he wanted to ask Dawson not to say anything to anybody until Mack had a chance to see what he could find out about Hannah Martin and her connection with the Delancey family. But he also wanted Dawson to check it out from his end, subtly, of course. It shouldn't be too hard to determine if Claire had borne a child and if that child had been a female named Stephanie.

HOYT DILLER SCRATCHED the back of his wrist. More than twenty years and the red dye in the tattoo still bothered him. He loved the tattoo. Had from the very beginning, when he and his old friend Marco Ficone had sat at Marco's kitchen table and designed it. It said everything. The red heart, the black letters spelling out *MOM* and especially the bullet-hole graphic in the center of the *O*. That had been his idea. He scratched at the red ink in the heart. It had itched from the first day. The tattoo artist had told him his body would get used to it. Now Marco, his friend and a fine gentleman, was long gone, Hoyt was working for Marco's oldest boy, Sal, who only cared about money, and the red ink on the back of his hand had faded, but it still itched.

He tapped a cigarette out of the pack on the dash. Just as he lit it, a white BMW pulled into the parking spot directly in front of Hannah Martin's motel room. The shiny German car was distinctly out of place in the dingy parking lot of the dingy motel. He unconsciously slid down in his seat as a tall man in a tailored sport coat and slacks got out of the car and pulled a cell phone from his pocket.

The sharp-dressed man stood for a moment behind the driver's-side door as he pretended to check the display and key in something with his thumbs. He was pretty good. It was almost impossible to see his head move as he checked out everything around him.

Hoyt smiled. The ploy worked so well it was almost a cliché. Pretending to text or talk made anyone look innocent and distracted while they scoped out a place or person.

Finally, apparently satisfied that no one was watching him, the man pocketed his phone, pulled out a key card and unlocked the room registered to Hannah Martin.

Now, that was interesting, Hoyt thought as he watched the man. His clothes were as expensive as Hoyt's own. Not the ridiculous T-shirt and black slacks the boss made his men wear on duty, but Hoyt's personal clothing. The suits he wore to the casinos and church. The linen pants

and rope sandals he liked to wear on vacation in the is-
lands.

The man didn't have on a tie, which made his coat
and slacks look a tad sloppy, but maybe he'd had a long
day. That wasn't the question, though. The question
was, what was he was doing at this no-tell motel in this
particular room?

Hoyt figured there were only two reasons a guy like
him would be at a place like this in the middle of the
afternoon. He was having a clandestine affair that he
dared not risk anyone finding out about—maybe with
a married woman. Maybe with a man.

But far more likely, considering where he'd parked,
right in front of Hannah Martin's motel room door,
he was exactly who Hoyt had been waiting for. He'd
hoped that Hannah would show up. He'd have grabbed
her and headed back to Galveston. But this could be
almost as good.

He called Mr. Ficone to report. "A guy just showed
up and went into the girl's room. He had the key card
in his pocket. From his clothes I figure he must be the
lawyer, Griffin. Your computer guy said court records
indicated that he bailed her out."

"Lawyer? Hell. Do you know how much I hate lawyers? What's he doing?"

"Can't tell from here. My guess, he's cleaning out
the room and checking out for her. Probably has her a
better place to stay."

"And what did you say his name is?"

"Griffin. I think his first name's Mack. I've got his
address, too. You want to send someone to check it out?
See if the girl's there?"

"Nah. I got nobody to spare. You handle it."

"I'll follow him. See where he goes. With any luck, he'll lead us to the girl."

"Can you get the drop on him while he's inside?"

"Sure I can, but my best bet is to stay hidden and then follow him—"

"No! He's a lawyer. I want him roughed up good. Right there in the motel. Get his thin lawyer blood all over the place. Grab his wallet, take his cash and leave the wallet there. Convince him you're gonna kill him for his money. But don't let him know how much you know. Act like you're all about the money."

"That's a big risk, Boss. This isn't a fancy place with interior entrances. Every single unit opens onto the parking lot. I don't think—"

"That's good, 'cause thinking's not what I pay you for. I pay you to do what I tell you *when* I tell you—and no arguments. Surprise him. Knock him on his pretty face. And ask him his name. If he's a lawyer, he's got a yellow stripe down his back. Scare him good, and while you're at it, don't forget we want him to think we ain't too bright."

No problem there, Hoyt thought wryly. "I don't know, Boss. What if he calls the cops?"

"What if he does? What are they going to do? You won't leave any evidence behind. Just make sure he doesn't see your face and make sure you leave him flat on the floor. Then let him call the cops while he's dragging himself up off the floor. You'll be hightailing it to his place to grab the girl. Then get back here as fast as you can. I got to meet with my suppliers tomorrow, which means either I've got the money or the drugs or that's all she wrote. That bitch better have the answer."

"Boss, let me talk to her. I can get her to spill what she knows. Besides, the rest of that shipment's probably somewhere around Dowdie, and that's a long way from Galveston."

"Campbell showed me a picture of her. I think I need to talk to her myself," Mr. Ficone said, his tone changing, becoming thick and rough. "She'll spill what she knows. I got my methods."

A shiver ran up Hoyt's spine. He'd seen the results of the boss's interrogation tactics a time or two, and he'd be happy if he never saw that again. Hoyt himself had done some cruel things a long time ago, back when he'd first started working for Marco. Back when he drank and took out his anger on whoever was closest—usually a girlfriend. He wasn't proud of that.

Now, though, he was an enforcer, a much cleaner, tidier job. Shooting somebody as part of his job wasn't a big deal. It wasn't personal, like other, closer methods.

"Sure, Mr. Ficone," Hoyt said. "All I was saying is if you bring her back to Galveston, then find out your stuff's up in Dowdie… Hell, that's six hours from this Chef Voleur place over to Galveston then another four to Dowdie. A straight shot, here to Dowdie, is only about seven hours. And like you said, time's getting short."

The boss grunted, a response he used like the Hawaiians use *aloha*. The trick was, his employees had the job of interpreting it. This time, Hoyt took it to mean that he still intended to question Hannah Martin himself.

Hoyt hadn't made three million dollars in the past five years, and remained alive, by disagreeing with the boss. He liked his job and his life. But Sal sometimes drove him nuts. For one thing, if he were the boss, he'd invest in some micro-tracking devices. Hell, if he had one, he could stick it on this guy's jacket when he attacked him.

Still, he did have Hannah's cell phone number, because he'd had the foresight to take Billy Joe Campbell's phone off his dead body.

Mr. Ficone's computer guy should be able to track Hannah through the GPS in her phone. Although Hoyt had no idea how all that high-tech stuff worked, he knew about it, thanks to his obsession with TV cop shows. In several episodes every season, somebody tracked somebody using the GPS on the person's cell phone.

While he waited to see what the guy with the Beemer would do, he called George, Mr. Ficone's computer guy.

"Got a question for you," he said. "I think I already know the answer."

After hanging up the phone, he got out of his car and walked over to the end of the building that housed the motel rooms. He sneaked down the far side and crossed through the breezeway nearest Hannah Martin's motel room.

In his mind, Hoyt was already in the fight. He was quick and intuitive, which, combined with his bulk and the element of surprise, made him almost unstoppable. He figured the attorney would be clumsy, as many long-limbed guys were. Piece of cake.

From his pocket, Hoyt dug out his brass knuckles. They were his favorite accessory, other than a handgun. The brass knuckles weren't as impersonal as a gun, but, like he'd reminded himself earlier, he tried not to question Mr. Ficone's motives.

Chapter Eight

Mack had been away from Hannah for twenty-three minutes. That was twenty-two minutes too long. What if she hadn't gone to sleep? What if she'd decided to head back to Dowdie on her own? He couldn't see her renting a car or finding the bus station in her exhausted state, but then she was awfully independent and determined for the type of woman he'd concluded she was. He'd locked the double dead bolt, but he'd also left the keys in the lock. His purpose was to keep others out, not lock her in. He'd hung his hopes on her exhaustion being as real as it seemed to be. He hoped he wouldn't regret not forcing her to come with him so he could keep an eye on her.

Once inside the motel room, what he saw cut into his heart. The space was small and shabby and smelled of disinfectant. He didn't want to think about what odors the disinfectant masked. The threadbare spread on the bed was undisturbed except for about twenty-four inches on the side near the bathroom, where the covers were barely mussed. It looked as if a child had slid into the far edge of the bed for warmth and comfort after being told not to muss it.

There was no suitcase, no hanging bag. He remembered what she'd sleepily muttered about keeping everything important in her purse and about how she'd jumped in the car and run. Still, it was sad to see nothing personal at all in the room. The closest thing to a personal item was a couple of discarded protein bar wrappers in the trash can.

He checked the bathroom where a wet washcloth and a damp towel hung on a bar. There was no toothbrush, no makeup kit and the faucet dripped.

Then he noticed the small photo stuck into the corner of the corroded mirror. It was the same photo she'd shown him.

His heart felt torn as he looked at the photo. He didn't want to touch it. Hannah had put it there as her one touch of home in this sad, decrepit motel where she'd hoped to get a few hours of sleep. Had she put the photo up because it comforted her? Or as a constant reminder that every hour she delayed getting back to Dowdie was another hour closer to death for her mother?

He reached for the photo, but his hand halted a couple of millimeters from it. What the hell? There was nothing sacred or magical about the picture. It was a snapshot, a frozen moment in time. Two girls sharing a happy, carefree afternoon.

He snatched up the picture with two fingers and turned it over. He'd seen the back when Hannah had first shown it to him and he remembered what was written there—by Hannah's mother and his own mom.

Swallowing against a lump in his throat, he stuck the photo in the pocket of his jacket. He was getting to know Hannah Martin better than he wanted to. From the moment he'd opened his door and seen her standing there, he hadn't gone more than a few moments without thinking about her.

The more he found out about her, the more he felt

responsible for her and the less he liked it. He stuck the photo in his shirt pocket, not wanting to look at it anymore. His reaction to it concerned him. He was going to be in big trouble if he didn't get away from her, the sooner the better. Which reminded him of the question that she had asked. Why had he jumped in and promised to secure her bail?

He glanced around the bathroom, even checking behind the door. There was nothing else of Hannah's in there. He took one more look around the pitiful room, touched the photo in his pocket and then tossed the key card onto the dresser.

He opened the door and glanced around the parking lot. Nothing seemed suspicious. There was one other car and three semitrailer trucks parked along the outside edges of the lot.

A couple in the unit across from Hannah's room were loading suitcases and baby things into the car, getting ready to leave. He watched them fasten the car seat into the back and place the baby in it. Once they'd driven away, he glanced around one more time, then reached behind him to pull the door closed.

That was when the train slammed into him. His rational brain knew it wasn't a train, but at the second of impact, that was the closest he could come to rationalizing what had happened.

The blow caused the inside of his head to explode in pain. It knocked him off his feet. He fell back against the open door and, despite his desperate scrambling, he stumbled backward and hit the floor butt first. He couldn't control his momentum, so the back of his head slammed against the floor.

He immediately tucked his legs and arms, preparing to roll up onto the balls of his feet. He heard the door swing shut, then felt a hand groping at his back pocket. He rolled and kicked and got a second stinging blow to the head. His roll and kick had left him with his feet under him, so he tensed, preparing to push himself up and at the bigger man, but before he could rise, a mass of hard muscle landed on top of him. A meaty forearm pressed into the back of his neck, effectively paralyzing him.

"Who are you?" a low voice muttered in his ear.

Mack's head pounded fiercely from the two blows, but he compartmentalized the pain. Without that skill, honed over a lifetime, the throbbing pain would overwhelm him and he'd be defenseless, writhing on the floor holding his head, leaving his attacker free to beat him, kill him or anything else he wanted.

With the pain locked away, Mack concentrated on the man's steady breathing, the stale odor of cigarettes and the detached competence that told him that for his attacker, this was not personal. The man was just doing his job. Mack filed that information away to think about later, along with an impression that didn't quite register in his conscious brain. An impression of red that felt as though it burned his eyes. He had no time to speculate on what his subconscious had noticed, though. He was too busy defending himself. He jabbed his elbow backward, aiming for his attacker's ribs. He got a soft grunt out of the guy for his trouble, but that wasn't enough. He'd barely hurt the beefier man.

He readied himself to jab the guy again, but before he could move, the other man grabbed a handful of Mack's hair and slammed his forehead into the floor. The blow was only slightly lessened by the thin layer of carpet, and Mack felt the skin split above his left eyebrow.

Warm blood trickled over his eyebrow and down his

upper eyelid. In a matter of seconds, the blood would be in his eye, blinding him with a red haze.

"I said, who are you and why are you in this particular room?" the man riding his back repeated. All he'd heard the first time were the words, but now, Mack recognized the voice. It was unmistakable. It was the man on Hannah's voice memo, the man who had killed Campbell and who knew Hannah could identify him.

Mack ignored the man's question. He needed to turn the tables fast. His head was splitting with pain. He could tell that one more well-placed blow might knock him out. And if one more drop of blood dripped in his eyes, he'd be rendered essentially blind. As the man groped Mack's butt again and got his fingers on his wallet, he shifted slightly, readying himself to buck like a mule to get the large man off his back.

The man felt him move and tensed. Before Mack could change tactics, and with surprising speed, the bigger man rose and stomped on the side of Mack's face with his heavy boot. He turned his foot first one way and then the other, as if grinding out a cigarette on Mack's cheek.

"Now, you listen to me," he said in the unmistakable low monotone of the recording on Hannah's phone. "We know you're hiding Hannah Martin. Where is she?"

"Who?" Mack grunted.

The shoe came down harder on Mack's cheek. Blood roared in his ears with an ominous whistling sound.

"Don't give me that. Why else would you be here? You want me to crush the side of your pretty face?"

Mack didn't answer. Every bit of strength, every ounce of concentration he had, was channeled into getting the better of this bull of a man.

Reaching backward, Mack wrapped his arm around

the ankle that was grinding into his cheek. It was an awkward position and if the man kicked backward, he could easily break Mack's shoulder.

Luckily, this time, Mack had surprise on his side, plus the agility of his lean muscles against the bulk of the other man. He jerked the ankle forward.

The burly attacker tipped to one side, off-balance. Mack got his arms and legs beneath him and pushed himself up to a crouch, but the other man righted himself with his hands against the closed door. He delivered a crushing kick to Mack's ribs. Mack collapsed in pain and breathlessness.

This time, the man stomped on Mack's neck.

"Maybe you don't get it," he huffed as he bent and pulled Mack's wallet out of his pants. Mack heard paper rustling, then the wallet landed a few inches in front of his nose.

"Nice to meet you Mr. Griffin. Nice to know where you live. I was hoping you'd cooperate. I'm going to be really pissed if I drive all the way to your house and she's not there."

"Then don't—waste your time," Mack grated through clenched teeth. "She's in—police custody." He coughed, which hurt his ribs, and spit out blood from a cut inside his cheek.

"Yeah? So what'd you waste all that bail for?"

"Not in jail," Mack muttered. He coughed again, groaning, hoping his ribs weren't broken. "Safe house. Don't know where." There was no way the man would believe such a bald lie. In fact, Mack was counting on him not believing it, counting on it making him angry.

"You lying—" the thug started as he lifted his foot to stomp on Mack's face again.

This time, Mack was ready. Each time the man lifted

his foot, he raised it too high. So for a split second, he was off-balance.

Mack twisted enough to grab the heavy boot with both hands. He grunted in satisfaction when he felt the thug's weight come down on that foot.

He jerked. The man toppled against the motel door.

At that instant somebody banged on the door. "Hey!" a man yelled. "What's going on in there?"

Mack didn't waste time wondering who it was. He whirled and pushed himself upright, ignoring the pain in his ribs, and crouched in a defensive stance. "Call the police!" he yelled back. He swiped his forearm across his forehead, where blood was dribbling down over his eyebrows.

His attacker rolled over and scrambled to get his feet under him. "Get away from the door!" he shouted. "I'll shoot you!"

"What?" came the response through the door. "This is my motel. You can't have a gun here. Open the damn door and stop fighting. Hell, I'm calling the police now!"

The big man lunged for the doorknob. Mack tried to focus on the man's face, but the blood was seeping into his eyes. He wanted to wipe his eyes again but he didn't have time.

His attacker threw open the door. Mack dived for his feet. He got hold of them, but the thug was pumping up momentum as he bulldozed over the motel owner, dragging Mack until Mack was forced to let go. He pulled his money clip, which his attacker hadn't found, out of his jacket pocket and peeled off three hundreds. "Sorry about the mess," he said, thrusting the bills at the guy, then turned and grabbed his wallet off the floor. "You okay?" he asked the motel owner.

But that man was picking up the money, cursing a

blue streak and digging in his pocket for his phone, all at the same time. Apparently he was fine.

Mack vaulted into his car and pulled out of the lot, breathing shallowly. He was pretty sure his ribs weren't broken, but they sure as hell were bruised. But his injuries would have to wait. He had to make sure the man didn't get to Hannah. He caught sight of the maroon car as it turned left, toward the interstate.

Good. Mack nodded as he maneuvered onto the street. The attacker was probably using GPS. Therefore, he'd be directed onto the interstate. So Mack turned and headed down the back roads, praying he could get to Hannah first.

He sped up as much as he could, considering the traffic. With one hand on the wheel, he grabbed his phone with the other and dialed Hannah's cell number. The phone rang until it went to voice mail.

"No!" he shouted, slamming his palm against the steering wheel. "Come on, Hannah. Wake up." He tried not to let himself think of another reason why she might not answer. "Be there," he whispered. He left a quick message for her to call him right away, then he dialed her number again. It rang once, twice, three times, four.

"Hannah, come on!" Mack growled. "Answer, damn it!"

"Hello?"

He blew out the breath he'd been holding. "Hannah!" he said, "Listen—"

"Mack? Is that you? I was asleep. How'd you know my number?"

"Hannah, listen to me. Get dressed. I'm on my way." He looked at his watch. It couldn't have been more than ten minutes since the man had sped out of the parking lot. They had about that much time left before he got to Mack's house.

"Go across the street to the pizza shop."

"Why? What's wrong?" Hannah's voice rose at least half an octave.

"Don't worry. Everything's going to be fine. Just get dressed and go—now! Don't waste any time."

"But—"

"Hannah, go!" he yelled, then remembered something. He'd dropped three hundreds on the motel floor. "Wait! Hang on. Do this first. Stay on the phone and go into my bedroom."

"Into your bedroom?"

"Yes. Just do it. Just listen to me and do what I tell you, okay?"

There was a pause. "Okay," she said. "I'm in the bedroom."

"Go to the closet. Stand in the doorway and run your hand along the left inside wall, next to the door facing all the way down to the baseboard."

"Okay," she said. Her voice sounded doubtful, worried. "Mack, all this is scaring me. Tell me what's going on."

"Did you find something on the inside wall?" he asked, ignoring her question.

"An outlet?" she asked.

"Right. It's fake. Pull on it and take out all the money that's in there. All of it. Put the money in your purse and then get out of there and go to the pizza shop."

"Okay," she said. He could hear her fingernails scratching on the plastic of the fake light switch. "Oh, my God!" she cried.

"What? What's wrong?"

"No-nothing. How much money is this?"

"Damn it, Hannah, it doesn't matter. Just take it and get out of there, please. There's no time to waste. Get out and go to the pizza shop. Wait for me there. Do not go anywhere else. Do not talk to anybody. Do you understand?"

"I— Yes, but—"

"Hannah! Do it!" He hung up the phone and stuck it in his pocket just in time to shift down into second and make a sharp turn. He drove for another ten minutes in hell, counting every second as he darted in and out of traffic.

He was terrified that she wouldn't do what he'd told her to. But he didn't dare call her again. He didn't want anything to delay her. Nor did he want to scare her even more than she already was.

When he got to his block on St. Charles, he turned left into the pizza shop parking lot. He threw the car into Park and left it running as he ran inside. There were several tables of people but no Hannah.

"Have you seen a young woman with a long, blond braid come in?" he asked the girl at the order counter.

"Whoa!" the girl at the counter said, looking horrified. "Mister, you're all—" she gestured "—like bloody. Are you okay?"

"I'm fine. The woman with the blond braid?"

The girl just stared at him. Her face was pale. She shook her head. "I don't—I mean—I'm going to get my manager."

"No," Mack said. "No. There's no need for that." He was aware of people at the tables looking at him and whispering. One child pointed at him and called out. "Daddy, look. That man's all bloody. Look! Did he get beat up?"

The girl disappeared through a door in the back.

"Damn it!" Mack said, looking around the shop. Where were the bathrooms? Maybe that was where Hannah was.

At that instant, the bell over the entrance rang. It was Hannah. His relief at seeing her quickly turned to annoyance. "Where have you been?" he snapped.

"Oh, my God!" Hannah stopped in her tracks, her hands flying to cover her mouth. "What happened to you? You look awful! Are you all right?"

"Yeah," he said, his tongue flicking out to touch the small split in his lower lip. "I ran into an admirer of yours at the motel."

Her face drained of color. "An admirer? I don't—"

He shook his head. "Sorry. Did I mention that I can be a sarcastic SOB?"

"You're saying somebody *attácked* you?" she blurted out.

The door behind the counter opened. "Hey, fellow," a short man in a striped pullover shirt came around the counter. "I don't know what kind of sicko fight club you're in, but you can't stay here. You're upsetting the customers."

Mack didn't acknowledge the man. He nodded at Hannah in answer to her question.

"At the motel?" Hannah said, the full meaning of his condition dawning on her. "*You* got beat up?"

"Come on," he said. "We've got to get out of here," he retorted, then shrugged gingerly. "He took me by surprise." He grabbed her hand. "Come on!" He pulled her out the side door to the BMW and opened the passenger door for her. "Get in," he said.

"Where are we going? I hope to the emergency room, because you need stitches." Her eyes roamed over his face. "Lots of them." She climbed into the passenger seat, and he slammed the door, ran around to the driver's side, got in and put the car in gear. He pulled out of the parking lot onto St. Charles and headed for the interstate.

"No. We don't have time for that."

"Don't be ridiculous," she said. "You have got to see a doctor. I mean, have you seen your face? It's—" She made a waving gesture toward him.

He shook his head. "Hannah, I said there's no time."

"Okay," she said. "How about you tell me what this is all about. Why all the superspy stuff?" She changed her voice to mock his deep rumble. *"Meet you in the pizza place. Bring all the money. Hurry. Don't ask any questions."*

"The guy who beat me up is on his way here to get you," Mack said flatly.

"What? To get me?"

"That's right. Whoever beat me up was looking for you. What I need to know is why."

"You're asking me?" Hannah said. "I don't know anything. I didn't know Billy Joe was selling drugs."

"Selling? That's not selling. Not with that much Oxy. He was distributing. Your mom's boyfriend was hooked up with some big nasty guys, in case you hadn't figured that out yet."

"I figured it out, thank you. The gunshot into Billy Joe's chest pretty much spelled that out for me." She yawned. "I asked you a question," she said sullenly.

"Yeah?"

She sighed in exasperation. "Are you going to go to a doctor? Because your face looks like—like somebody stomped on it."

"Thanks," he muttered, but he lifted his head and glanced in the rearview mirror. "Damn," he whispered.

He did look like somebody had stomped all over his face. He hardly recognized himself. Splitting his attention between the road and the mirror, he cataloged his injuries. There was that nasty cut over one brow that had left a trail of blood running down his eyelid and into his eye, tingeing everything red. The white of his left eye was bloodshot and the skin around it was puffy and beginning to turn red. He was going to have a black eye.

He touched his brow, near the cut. "That's probably going to leave a scar," he said.

"Oh, you think?" Hannah responded sarcastically. She dug into her purse. "I've got some hand wipes in here somewhere," she said. "Oh, here." She dug out a wad of cash. "Here's your money."

"Keep it for now," he said.

She shrugged and stuffed it back into her purse. "Fine. You want me to try to clean your face a little? I'm surprised you can see anything with all that blood in your eyes."

He blinked and felt the dried blood on his eyelids pull at his skin. "Hang on," he said as he came up to the entrance onto the I-10. He downshifted and looked at the signs, wondering what to do.

Should he go east or west? If they went east, all they'd be doing was running. Going west would take Hannah back the way she'd come—back to Dowdie, Texas. Back to danger. But he was with her. He could protect her, he hoped. He sure didn't want to turn the other direction and doom her to running for the rest of her life. He couldn't live with himself if he allowed her to do that. Trying not to imagine what Teilhard would say and how loud he would say it when he found out Mack had taken her out of the jurisdiction, he turned west.

Hannah found the hand wipes, extracted one and reached over to clean his temple.

"Give me that," he said, taking the wipe from her. He kept one hand on the wheel as he rubbed his right eye, then his left. "Ouch, that burns," he said, looking in the rearview mirror again. His nose was bleeding and his right cheek looked as though it had been dragged across a basketball court. He carefully dabbed at his nose. "I guess I scared the people at the pizza shop, didn't I?"

"That's an understatement. You definitely scared me. I almost had a heart attack when I saw you." She looked out the window. "Where are we going? Why are we headed west?"

"Here," Mack said, ignoring her question. He pulled out his phone and handed it to her. "Take a look at the picture I took at the motel."

"I asked you a question," she said while she was pulling up the picture on his phone's screen. "Wait. What is this?"

"See the maroon car? That's the guy who attacked me. Can you see the driver? Does the car look familiar?"

She flicked her fingers to zoom in. "Oh," she gasped.

"What? You recognize the car?"

"I'd forgotten all about it. The day Billy Joe was murdered, there was a car parked at the curb about half a block away from the house. It might have been this color.

"I think it is the car, but I can't see the driver." Her voice was shrill and breathy. "So he's the man who beat you up?"

"Could you stop saying that? I got in a few really good blows, too. It was kind of a tie."

"A tie," Hannah repeated. "So he looks as bad as you do?"

Mack ignored her.

"What did he look like?"

"He wasn't real tall," Mack said, "but he was huge and muscled. His arms were like hams and he had on a tight T-shirt, like an arrogant weight lifter might wear. Brown hair, really thin on top. I couldn't get a good look at his face. I was too busy."

She took a short, sharp breath. "The man who shot Billy Joe was wearing a tight shirt."

Mack nodded grimly. "So that is him. What do you have that they want, Hannah?"

She looked at him sidelong. "I don't know."

"Come on, Hannah. From what you told me, it sounds like Billy Joe convinced them that you know where the rest of the drugs are."

"I don't. I didn't know anything about drugs," she said.

"Why do you think they're after you, then? Billy Joe stole money and drugs. Let's assume for a moment that you really didn't notice that your mother's boyfriend was transporting and selling drugs. Yet Billy Joe somehow managed to make Ficone's man believe that you have the missing money, or at least know where it is."

"But I don't. That's ridiculous."

"Tell me everything he gave you."

"Me?" she repeated with a laugh. "Billy Joe never gave me anything. I mean, he wasn't big on presents anyway, but occasionally he'd bring Mom something."

"Like what?"

"Well, one day after he got back from a *business trip,* he brought her a bottle of very expensive cologne."

"Is it at your house?"

She nodded. "The bottle is. It's empty, because he got mad and poured the cologne down the toilet."

"What else?"

"He said he was going to buy her a car, but he never did. Oh. He gave her a topaz pendant once. I don't think it was real. Mom and I both thought the stone was too large and gaudy, but he insisted she wear it."

"Where is it?" Mack said.

Hannah frowned. "I don't know. She might have it on. Now, will you please tell me why we're going west? Where are you taking us. To Dowdie?"

"Absolutely," he said.

"Really?"

The way her face lit up made his heart ache.

"Oh, thank you, Mack. You're going to help me find my mother."

"We're going to Dowdie," he repeated, "because we've got to find the rest of Billy Joe's drugs and money before Ficone's man tracks you down and kills you."

MACK TURNED HIS entire attention to the road. He read the signs for upcoming towns. Very few of them were familiar, but then he hadn't done much traveling by car west of the New Orleans area. He looked over at Hannah, who was slumped against the window, sound asleep. He was glad. She was so exhausted, and she probably hadn't gotten eight hours total since she'd driven in from Dowdie.

Her eyes were twitching, which meant she was dreaming. Mack didn't have to wonder what kind of dreams she was having. Her mobile face told him everything as it morphed from serene to nervous, from relaxed to fearful as she navigated her way through the dreams. He hated to see fear darkening her expression. He wanted her to be happy, not sad. Relaxed, not frightened. But no matter the expression, her face was so lovely it made his heart ache.

What was he doing, taking her right back into danger? He should have given Teilhard all the information he had and turned Hannah over to him to put her in protective custody. Teilhard, with all the resources he had at his disposal, could protect her. Mack knew he couldn't.

He'd rejected law enforcement for the same reason he couldn't be a defense lawyer. He took people's pain, emotional and physical, too personally, not to mention that he was constantly worried that he wouldn't be able to help them. It was the same old doubt and fear that he'd carried with him his entire life. But this time, even with the doubts and fears, he'd committed to keeping Hannah safe, and that scared him. The only other time he'd pledged a commitment to keep a woman safe, he'd failed, and the woman—his mother—had died.

Hannah deserved someone better. Too bad he was all she had.

He glanced over at her and to his surprise, she opened her sleepy eyes and smiled at him, then closed them again.

Mack kept an eye on her as he drove, amazed that she could be so frightened yet sleep so peacefully. He wished he were the kind of man who could inspire that kind of trust. *I promise I'll protect you,* he thought, *with my life.*

Mack arched his neck, trying to get rid of the nagging headache he'd had ever since the man who'd ambushed him had slammed his head into the floor. He must have moaned aloud because Hannah started, then opened her eyes and sat up, yawning.

"What's the matter?" she asked.

"Nothing. My head hurts a little."

"That place above your eyebrow is turning into a lump," she said, "so it's no wonder it hurts. How did you let him get the drop on you, anyhow?" Hannah asked.

Mack glared at her. "First of all, I didn't *let* him. And like I told you, he surprised me. I came out of the motel room and was just about to lock the door and head back to my car when something hit me like a freight train, right in the throat. I think he must have swung at me with his forearm. I twisted around and went down. I don't think I've ever been hit so hard in my life."

"You didn't see anything?" she asked.

"Anything like what?" he asked. "I told you, I face-planted and before I had a chance to turn over, much less get up, he jumped on top of me. I think he was using brass knuckles." He tongued a deep cut on the inside of his lip that matched the one on the outside, then pulled his lip down and strained to get a look at the damage in the rearview mirror.

As he rubbed his jaw where one of the man's blows had landed, a vague impression he'd gotten during the fight came back to him. He looked down at his hands on the steering wheel, then stretched out his right hand and examined the back of it for a second.

"The only thing I noticed was that there was something on the back of his hand," he said. "Something that looked—" He stopped cold. His stomach flipped over and his scalp burned. Had there really been anything on the man's hand, or was the image a weird trick of the blood obscuring his vision? He shook his head, trying to clear it. The only other explanation was that he was having a flashback to his childhood, brought on by the sight of blood and a raging man swinging his fists.

Hannah put her hand on his. "Oh, right. The red tattoo."

"What?" Mack said, as his brain slowly processed what she had said. His heart felt like a solid block of ice in his chest as his brain plummeted back in time to the worst night of his life. The night his worst nightmare had come true. "Red tattoo?" he rasped.

"What's the matter?" Hannah asked. "You look like you've seen a ghost."

He shook his head. "Nothing. I'm fine. It was probably the blood in my eyes."

She took her hand away and folded her arms, shrinking back into the passenger seat. "The man who shot Billy Joe had a tattoo on his hand. It was red."

Mack didn't know how his frozen heart was managing to pump blood through his veins—even if it did feel like ice water. His hands tightened on the steering wheel until they cramped. And his brain was racing. He wasn't sure he wanted to hear what Hannah was about to say. Despite his uncertainty, his numb lips formed the questions, "Where? What kind of tattoo?"

"It was on the back of his right wrist." she started, then swallowed audibly. Her voice was shaky with remembered fear when she continued. "A red heart, with the letters *M-O-M* inside it. And inside the *O* was something that looked like…" She paused.

Mack took a deep breath through lungs that felt as though they were filled with broken glass. "A bullet hole. Right through the center of the *O,*" he finished for her.

Chapter Nine

Hoyt cursed and yawned as he turned right on St. Charles Street for the second time. It was late, after eight o'clock at night. As soon as he'd gotten on the interstate to race to Mack Griffin's house, he'd realized his mistake. Within five minutes it was backed up with rush-hour traffic. Then a tractor-trailer rig carrying PVC pipe turned over and the pipe rolled everywhere, blocking all lanes. He was stuck, practically not moving at all, for over two hours.

He just hoped Griffin was behind him and experiencing the same frustrating delay. The bad news, even if he was behind him, was that he could call Hannah and warn her—tell her to run and hide.

When he'd finally made it to Griffin's address, he'd driven by slowly, trying to see if he could tell whether Griffin was there and more important, whether Hannah was there.

If she was here, he'd manage one way or another to get in and grab her, hopefully before Griffin got home.

He wasn't looking forward to another fistfight. Even with his brass knuckles, the younger, fitter man had almost beaten him.

As HOYT PASSED Griffin's house, he noticed the pizza shop directly across St. Charles. At the last second he whipped across the median and into its parking lot. Stepping inside, he went up to the counter, where two waitresses in T-shirts with the pizza shop's logo and towels over their shoulders were talking.

"And then Tom kicked him out," the first waitress said. "I'm telling you, Kelly, he looked awful. His face was all bloody."

"I'm Detective Norris," Hoyt interrupted with a friendly smile. "Someone called about a disturbance?"

"Yeah!" the first waitress said. "My boss must have called. A man with blood all over him came in here looking for someone. He looked like a-an ax murderer."

The other waitress laughed nervously.

"What about the woman?" Hoyt said casually, patting his shirt pocket as if looking for a pen and pad.

"The woman? Oh, she came in right about the time my boss came out. She was blond with a long braid in back. She looked scared."

"Where did they go when Tom threw them out?"

"They got in his car and drove off."

Hoyt took a step forward. "What kind of car?"

"White. A BMW, maybe?" the young woman said. "You probably want to talk to Tom."

"That's okay," Hoyt said, pulling out his cell phone as if he was about to call for backup. "I know the car. Thanks. You've been real helpful." Then he ran out of the shop and jumped into his car, slamming his palm against the steering wheel.

How had Griffin beaten him here? He must have taken a shortcut on some backstreets.

His best guess was that Griffin was probably either on the interstate by now, headed east, away from any danger to Hannah, or that he'd headed toward the bayou country. He couldn't imagine that the lawyer was helping her merely out of the goodness of his heart or his sense of justice. Griffin was probably in love with her, or at least in lust, and hoping to keep her and himself out of danger.

It was a damn shame he didn't have a way of tracking them. If he were the boss, he'd pay for micro-tracking devices. He could have stuck one on Griffin's expensive sport coat during the fight.

Then it hit him.

HANNAH SLEPT WHILE Mack drove for another couple of hours, doing his best to ignore the headache that had been getting worse every minute since Hannah had described the red tattoo that had haunted his dreams for almost twenty years.

He massaged his left temple, where the pain had settled, and winced. His vision seemed to be getting blurry, too. The halos of oncoming headlights were growing bigger and brighter by the minute.

He glanced over at Hannah, wanting to wake her up and ask her more about the man and his tattoo, but truthfully, he wasn't sure he wanted to know any more. At least not right now. He needed to digest what she'd already told him.

That red-and-black image was a symbol of everything it had taken him years to bury in the back of his mind. The thought of dredging all that up and trying to deal with it again made him physically sick.

What were the odds that two men in the world had the exact same tattoo in the exact same place?

He swallowed against the acrid taste that always seemed to accompany these bad headaches and pushed the tattoo back into the lockbox where he kept the unbearable memories. But locking the image away didn't help the headache. That plus the beating he'd taken and the painful glare from oncoming headlights all combined to make it impossible for him to drive any farther.

About a half hour after they passed through Shreveport, Mack exited the interstate onto a state road and drove about eleven miles, passing through a couple of small towns until he came to one that was big enough to have a Piggly Wiggly, a Walmart and, surprisingly, two motels. He stopped at the Walmart, figuring he'd get them some toiletries and pajamas and underwear. As soon as he stopped the car, Hannah woke up, so he gave her money to do her own shopping. He got himself a small bottle of ibuprofen, which he opened on the spot. He downed two of the tablets with a bottle of water from a vending machine, then put the bottle in his pocket. While he waited for Hannah to finish shopping, Mack called Dawson again, since he hadn't called him back. The phone rang again and again and again.

"Damn it, Delancey," Mack muttered just as Dawson answered. *Well, finally.* "Where have you been?"

"Jules and I took a raft trip. We camped overnight and there was no phone service. We're driving back now. I was going to call you in the morning."

"Remember the young woman that came to see me while you and I were on the phone the other day? She's in some trouble because of her mom's boyfriend."

"Yeah? What kind of trouble?"

"You know what? Forget that. What's important is, I found a letter in her purse. The envelope was sealed, but it wasn't mailed. It was from her mother. I opened it." Mack paused for a fraction of a second, waiting for Dawson to give him hell about tampering with other people's things, but he didn't. So Mack continued. "The mother's name is Stephanie Clemens. Have you ever heard that name?"

"Not that I recall. Who is she?"

Mack took a deep breath.

"What's going on, Mack?" Dawson asked, beginning to sound slightly concerned with a pinch of impatience.

"I'm getting to it. The letter, like I said, is from mother to daughter. Stephanie Clemens has liver disease and is on dialysis. The letter is one of those confessions before dying."

"Okay." Dawson sounded distracted.

"Daw, Stephanie Clemens claims she's Claire Delancey's daughter."

"What?" Dawson snapped. Mack had his attention now.

"Does your great-aunt Claire have a daughter?"

"Not—" Dawson paused. "I've heard that she originally went to France because she was pregnant. She ended up staying there for ten years the first time she went. When she came back to Chef Voleur, she was around twenty-six and she didn't have a child with her."

"That would have been too long ago, anyhow. This woman is forty-two and Hannah is twenty-five."

"Aunt Claire went back to France in—let's see. She was probably thirty-six or so. And now she's seventy-nine."

Mack added in his head. "That would work. Is there somebody you could ask other than your family? It would be good if you kept this to yourself for a while. I'd hate to hurt your family if this is just a scam."

"I agree. Aunt Claire was always the *bad girl* of the family. She's lived *in sin* with Ektor Petrakis, the wealthy Greek businessman, in France all these years. He died recently, which is why she's returning here.

And yes, you're right about keeping it from the family until we're sure. I'll do some research on my great-aunt and see what I can find."

"Thanks. I'm not convinced that Hannah is any kin to your illustrious family yet."

"Do you think she's trying to get money?"

"Not Hannah. I don't think she has any idea what the letter says. She was carrying it but she hadn't opened it. The flap hadn't been touched."

Mack saw Hannah rolling a shopping cart toward him. "I've got to go. I'll give you a call maybe tomorrow if I have any more information."

"Okay. Meanwhile, I'll see what I can come up with on this end. Stephanie Clemens, right? What's the girl's name?"

"Hannah Martin. Got to go. Thanks, Dawson."

Mack and Hannah put their purchases in the car and Mack headed toward the motels. By the time he got them checked into the nicer of the two motels, Hannah was asleep again. He roused her gently, then grabbed the Walmart bags and unlocked the small room, which wasn't much better than the one Hannah had rented in Metairie. He set the bags on the dresser next to the old-fashioned TV as Hannah came in. He opened his mouth to ask her which of the two double beds she wanted, but before he even got the first word out she'd disappeared into the bathroom, her shopping bags in her hands.

That was fine with him. He took a six-pack of soft drinks out of a bag and stuck it into the small refrigerator. Taking the half-empty water bottle with him to the bed closest to the door and farthest from the bathroom, he took a good, long swig, then flopped down onto the bed and threw one arm over his eyes.

"Ow," he muttered, immediately taking his arm

away. His face was way too sore for that. His head still pounded and the ibuprofen tablets hadn't helped his nausea any. He propped himself up on his elbow and drank some more water, this time slowly, then lay back down and closed his eyes.

Behind his closed lids, the memory he'd tried to lock away burned through his eyelids like heat lightning. A big man—as big as Goliath—was there, his hamlike fists were doubled and his face purple and distorted with rage. There was another person in the room. A woman crouched on the floor against the wall with a terrified look on her blood-streaked face. She was crying and shouting, "Run, Mackie! Run to Aunt Beth's house."

Mack felt as though he were watching a movie on a big screen. There, in the foreground of the shot, a boy, no more than twelve, yelled, "Leave my mom alone!" The Goliath ignored the child, except for a vicious snarl in his direction as he advanced on the woman.

The boy's line of sight was nearer to the big man's hands than his face. So the prominent black-and-red tattoo on the back of the man's hand was no more than a couple of feet from his face. To him, the ugly, crooked red heart with the word *MOM* spelled out in black letters was an obscene insult to his mother.

Then the man clenched his fists and the tattoo seemed to stretch until the *O* in *MOM* stood out. The boy stared at it. Finally, he made out what was drawn in the middle of the *O*. It was a bullet hole.

The boy took all this in during the few seconds while the giant was advancing on his mother, cursing and yelling and threatening her if she didn't get up. By the time he loomed over her, reaching for her with that huge, tattooed hand, the boy went into motion. He ran at the man, swinging his arms. He hit him over and over, crying, "Leave her alone, leave her alone."

Finally, the man backhanded the boy, sending him tumbling to the floor. Then he grabbed him by the arm and jerked him to his feet, and Mack heard the man's low, threatening voice. "If you try that again, your mom will end up a lot more bloody than she is now. Understand?"

The boy swung at him again. The man flung him against the wall while the mother screamed, "Run, Mackie, run!" Sweat formed on Mack's forehead and dripped into his hair as he remembered what happened next.

It took more effort than he'd expected, but he finally managed to open his eyes and sit up. Yet still, even though he saw the front window and door of the motel room, part of the vision remained—the image of a red heart with the word *MOM* in black with a bullet hole through the middle of the *O*.

He wiped his face and pressed his fingertips against his temples and squeezed his eyes shut, pushing as hard as he could to force the awful memory away.

At that moment, the bathroom door opened, releasing a cloud of steam into the room, and Hannah stepped through it like a water sprite from a misty lake.

"Oh," she said on a huge sigh. "I feel so much better."

Mack stared, thankful to have something beautiful to look at after all that horror. She had on pink-and-purple pajama pants and a little pink top with tiny straps holding it up. Her hair was wet and long and hung over one shoulder in cascading waves, and her cheeks were dewy and pink. She smiled at him, and his heart, which he'd have sworn was cold and shattered into a million pieces, began to warm up and heal. Goose bumps rose on his arms. He wasn't quite sure why.

He didn't know where to look, since every single inch of her was fresh and lovely and clean, so he pushed himself up off the bed. When he stood, he swayed as light-headedness came over him for a second and the edge of his vision turned dark. But it faded almost immediately.

"Mack, are you okay? You look pale," Hannah said.

"Sure," he answered quickly. "I'm fine. I'm just going to unpack." He carefully walked over to where he'd set the plastic shopping bags on the TV table. He'd bought underwear, a pair of Levi's, a couple of T-shirts, white socks, an inexpensive pair of jogging shoes, disposable razors, deodorant and a comb. "Damn it, I didn't think about luggage," he muttered.

"I'll bet you didn't think about your face, either," she said.

He held up the razors.

She laughed and shook her head. "Not exactly what I'm talking about," she said with exaggerated patience. "You probably won't be able to use those for a couple of days. Here." She handed him one of her bags, which was damp from the shower spray.

When he looked inside, he remembered. "Oh, right," he said, as he checked the contents. Rubbing alcohol. Bandages in several sizes. Sterile reinforced strips and a tube of antibiotic ointment.

She took the bag back and grabbed his hand. "Sit over here," she said, guiding him to a hard-backed chair in front of the dresser.

"Let me take a shower first," he said, trying to maneuver away from her and toward the bathroom. He definitely needed a shower, but not as much as he needed to get away from her. He was still queasy from the dream/memory and still fascinated with how lovely she was, fresh from her shower. He couldn't tell if his racing pulse was caused by nausea or lust.

"Okay," she said, smiling at him. "Try to get all that dried blood off while you're in there, but hurry. Otherwise I might be sound asleep."

Once Mack had disappeared into the bathroom, Hannah sat down on her bed with a pillow propped behind her head. She felt warm and clean and drowsy after her hot shower. She'd almost drifted off to sleep when Mack opened the bathroom door. Hannah opened her eyes to a narrow slit and peeked at him. He wore nothing but a pair of pale blue pajama pants from Walmart. He stood in the doorway for a moment, backlit by the bathroom light. His hair was wet and furrowed, as though he'd raked his fingers through it. His body was sprinkled with droplets of water that shimmered in the reflection from the bathroom, making him look covered in stardust.

She saw that he was just as trim and finely muscled as she'd suspected he was from the cut of his clothes. He had broad shoulders and a lean waist, trim hips and, if she could judge by what she could see of the fit of the pajama pants, long, powerful thighs.

After a few seconds, she realized he was studying her. She didn't move a muscle, not even a twitch of her eyelid. He didn't move either, didn't change his neutral expression as his gaze assessed her. Then, when she thought she couldn't go another second without wiggling something, even if it was nothing but her big toe, he brushed both hands over his wet hair and flung the droplets of water at her. "Wake up, sleepyhead," he said.

"Hey!" she cried, wiping her face and chuckling. "What are you doing?"

He smiled, surprising Hannah. "Hey, yourself. Just checking to see if you were asleep. Time to dress my wounds. Get up."

She faked a yawn that immediately stretched into a real one. "They're fine, I'm sure. I think I'm going to turn over and go back to sleep."

"No problem. I'll take care of all this myself. Where'd you put the bandages?"

"Oh, no, you don't. I'll do it. You sit right there." She got up, pointing to the single hard-backed chair. "I need to see how bad those cuts and scrapes are."

Mack shrugged. "Yes, sir, Dr. Martin." He sat as she gathered up the supplies she'd bought. There was a mirror over the dresser, and seeing his reflection, he was startled all over again by the condition of his face. "Damn it," he said.

"What?" Hannah called from the bathroom, over the sound of running water.

"The bathroom mirror was foggy, but I can see my face now and it hurts."

She came back into the room with a steaming washcloth. "You might be more comfortable lying down. I'm going to put this over your face and I want it to stay there for a couple of minutes."

He was tempted, but he figured since Hannah was going to be leaning over him in that skimpy little pajama top, he wasn't sure he could control himself. Sitting up, he'd be better able to hide any physical evidence of that lack of control.

"Why do you even need that? I just got out of the hot shower."

"I just want to be sure all the scabs are soft." She set

the items on the dresser in front of him and told him to lean his head back. "Are you sure you don't want to lie down?" she said.

"Damn sure."

"Why?"

Mack opened an eye and peered at her. "Why what?"

"You said *damn sure.*"

"I said that?" He hadn't realized he'd said the words out loud.

"Yeah. But I don't see why you wouldn't. It would take the strain off your neck."

Right, but it might add strain somewhere lower down. As soon as the thought flitted through his mind, he glanced at Hannah, but she hadn't reacted, so he must not have said that one aloud.

"Okay, then. Tilt your head back."

He did and she applied the hot cloth.

He moaned.

"Am I hurting you?" she asked as her fingers smoothed and straightened the soft, hot cloth.

"No," he said on a sigh. "Moan of pleasure."

"Is the cloth dripping too much?"

"Nope. Not at all. It's great," he said, hearing the strain in his voice.

"Good. Now stay still." The light, teasing touch of her fingers sent thrills through all the tiny nerves of his body as she slid them around the side of his face and then to the back of his neck where, to his dismay, she massaged for a few seconds. The more she kneaded the muscles of his neck, the closer he came to embarrassing himself.

"I hope your neck isn't too sore. I still think you ought to lie down."

"No!" he snapped, then cleared his throat. "I'm fine."

Her fingers caressing the nape of his neck were about to drive him crazy. When had that area become so sensitive? Maybe it had always been. For the life of him, right at this moment he couldn't remember another woman ever touching him there.

"Okay," she said, taking her hand away. "I'm going to get the bandages and the sterile strips ready. Then I'm going to use a hot soapy cloth to clean your face."

Mack nodded slightly. Even with his neck tilted back, he was becoming so relaxed that he was about to drift off to sleep. "If you don't hurry up I may go to sleep and slide out of the chair."

"That's okay. I'll just take care of you on the floor," she said, a smile in her voice.

He spent the next couple of minutes trying to stop imagining how Hannah would go about *taking care of him on the floor*.

Chapter Ten

"Okay," Hannah said. "Your face is finally clean of blood. Now I can get to work."

Mack was grateful for her matter-of-fact statement. It helped him concentrate on something besides how she might take care of him on the floor.

"How do you know so much about first aid?" he asked once she finally took the washcloth off his face and he could straighten his neck. He winced. His neck was stiff and sore. Very sore. Probably from that thug bashing his forehead into the floor.

"This is not just first aid. Some of it is second aid." She smiled. "I was a lifeguard at the lake for three summers. I've handled my share of small emergencies."

Mack assessed her. "Ever dealt with a big emergency?"

She shook her head. "The worst thing I saw was a kid jump off the tall diving board and land on the low board. I didn't have to do anything, though. Someone called 911 and an ambulance came. The head lifeguard helped out in the meantime."

"What happened to the kid?"

"I think he bruised or severed his spinal cord. I didn't know him or his parents but I think the last I heard, they'd taken him to Dallas." She examined the cut over his eyebrow. "I'm going to use sterile strips on this. I need to pull the edges of the skin together." She touched his brow.

"Ow," he said, pulling away.

"You're going to have a nice bruise there. What did he do? Slam your head against the wall?"

"Floor." Embarrassed, he dropped his gaze.

"Oh." Hannah's face was about a foot from his. She touched an uninjured spot under his chin and urged his head up. "Sorry," she said. "Bad attempt at a joke."

He lifted his gaze to hers. For a moment, neither one of them spoke. Mack felt like this was a crossroads of some kind, as if what he did in the next second would change their relationship irrevocably.

But he had no idea what he should do. No. He *knew* what he should do. His problem was, he *knew* what he wanted to do. He wanted to kiss her. He was dying to find out if those vulnerable lips were as soft and sexy to the touch as they were to look at. But the part of his brain that was still rational was screaming, *Don't do it. She's everything you don't want.*

Before he could act on that excellent advice, her eyes changed. They went from clear blue to smoky and dark. Her gaze flickered down to his mouth and he forgot to breathe. Was she about to take the decision out of his control?

But instead of leaning forward and kissing him, she caught her lower lip between her teeth and blinked. "Okay, then. I—need to clean this cut on your brow with alcohol," she said. "It's probably going to sting." She soaked a corner of a washcloth in alcohol, then placed it against the cut.

"Ow!" he said. "That stings."

"I know," she said seriously. "Hence my recent state-ment regarding stinging."

Mack chuckled.

She began to gently scrub the cut and damn it, it did hurt. He sat still, his jaw tensed, as she finished with his brow and went to the cut on his lip, the scrape on his cheek, which stung even more, and a small cut in-side his nostril.

Trying to take his mind off the stinging, not to men-tion the torture of seeing her fresh, lovely skin so up close and personal, he took the opportunity to survey her features. She wasn't exactly pretty. Her high cheek-bones, defined jawline and small chin made her look stubborn, unless she was smiling. Her small nose kept her from looking too stern, and her wide eyes looked positively innocent, if you ignored the jawline.

She poured more alcohol and went back to cleaning the cuts and scrapes.

Mack couldn't make himself stop looking at her mouth. It was soft and turned up at the corners, not at all stern. It was that jaw that was the problem, although if she was completely relaxed, for instance when she slept, it softened a lot. As she worked, she bit her lower lip. Mack felt a stirring of desire inside him at the sight of her small, white teeth. He allowed himself a fleet-ing daydream of what it would be like to make love to her. He decided it would be very, very nice, but it would never happen.

"I'm done, I think," Hannah said, looking down into Mack's eyes.

He didn't say anything and he didn't move. He didn't dare. Her mouth was so close to his that all he had to do was raise his head a half inch and their lips would touch.

Her eyes were soft and her mouth was the sexiest

thing he'd ever seen. Just about the time he made the momentous decision to steal a kiss, she retreated.

"Okay," she said, too briskly. "There you are. I don't know how much better you look, but you're going to feel a lot better."

He cleared his throat and sat up. The beginnings of arousal faded as he set his mind to ignoring the sensation.

"Ah, hell," he muttered. "I forgot to buy a toothbrush," he said. "Damn it!"

Her eyes sparkled. "Nyah-hah-hah!" she said, twirling an imaginary mustache. Reaching into one of the bags, she pulled out two toothbrushes and a tube of toothpaste.

"You're a regular Boy Scout, aren't you?" he said.

"That's *Girl Scout* to you," she retorted, "in case you can't tell."

Mack's control dissolved like tissue in the rain. The dangerous sensations he'd finally managed to suppress roared to life. He willed himself to stop, but there were some temptations too difficult to resist and right at that moment, with Hannah so near, her cheeks as pink as the little top she wore, she was the embodiment of temptation.

"Oh, I can tell," he said, and even though he was trying to stoke the fires of resistance, his hand reached out and touched her flaming cheek. "I can tell."

She didn't move a muscle while the backs of his fingers brushed her hot skin, or when he pulled his hand back and lifted his gaze to hers. But when he stared into her eyes and ran his forefinger across the curve of her bottom lip, she did move. She lifted her face to his in silent invitation for him to touch her again.

"Hannah," he said, shaking his head slowly. "You don't want me to—"

Her chin rose another fraction of an inch and her heavy-lidded gaze met his. "Are you telling me what I want?" she asked, her tone a mixture of amusement and challenge.

"I just don't think this is—"

"What? A good idea? I can't really think in terms of good or not good right now." She angled her head slightly. "I'm tired and scared and worried, and tomorrow I'm sure I'll have regrets, but tonight I just want a few minutes of being held and cherished and…" The longer she talked, the softer and more sultry her voice became, until she was whispering, her lips so close to his that he could feel the air stirring with her breaths.

Then, before his desire-soaked brain could think of a way to convince her just how bad an idea this was, she kissed him. At first it was butterfly soft, barely brushing his lips. If he'd had his eyes closed, he might have thought he'd imagined it.

He waited, craving and dreading what she was going to do next.

She kissed him a little harder and a little harder, until she was pressing her mouth insistently against his and he was fast losing the ability to breathe evenly. Then she pulled back. "You know, Mack, I'd have made you as a player. What's the matter? Got some kind of lawyer rule against kissing a client? Or just too tired?"

He swallowed, unsure how to answer her. The thing was, he *was* a player—when the game was being played by his rules, which this game was not.

He allowed himself a small smile at her brazen challenge. Here was his way out. He'd steal the game from her and show her what being a player actually meant. It would terrify her and she'd back off. At that thought, his desire was already waning.

Watch out, Miss Martin, he said to himself. *This game's about to change.*

"Well?" she taunted, the mischief edging out the embarrassment in her eyes. She obviously felt very sure of herself at this moment.

"You don't know what you're doing," he said softly, the smile still in place.

A brief shadow crossed her face. "What do you mean?" she asked, feigning innocence.

He lifted his head and looked down his nose at her. "Oh, it's not your fault. You've only had boys to play with. It's understandable that you don't know what you're getting into by flirting with a man. I'd advise you to stop now."

"Stop?" she said as a flush rose from her neck all the way up to her cheeks. "I—don't want to stop."

"Okay, then," he said. Without taking his gaze from hers, he slid his hands in a caress up her arms to her shoulders. Then, without changing expression, he gave a flick of his fingers and pushed the tiny straps of her top down off her shoulders until the swell of her breasts was the only thing keeping it from slipping to her waist.

Hannah gasped as she felt the material slipping farther and farther down toward the tips of her breasts, tickling as it slid. "What—" she started, but she stopped herself when Mack's smile grew noticeably wider. She'd started this, and she was not about to be the one who chickened out. She lifted her face to his and touched his lips with hers.

"Is that all you've got?" she whispered against his lips. She heard the breathy nervousness in her voice, but with any luck, Mack's blood was rushing in his ears and he hadn't heard it.

"That's not even a taste," he muttered, sliding his

mouth from her lips to her chin, then to her jaw and along the jawline all the way to her earlobe.

Her shaky breathing threatened to turn into a complete inability to breathe at all. He bit down lightly on her earlobe and she gasped as a sharp thrill fluttered through her all the way to the center of her desire.

He whispered something that she didn't quite catch, then he wrapped his arms around her, pulled her to him and kissed her fully and deeply. She did forget how to breathe. But Mack was breathing for her, feeding her breath and life, along with an arousal so acute that she could scarcely stand it as he opened his mouth and teased her lips with his tongue.

Nothing Hannah had ever done with the boys she'd dated had prepared her for this—this total immersion into the erotic fire of a true, deep kiss. She'd been kissed before. But Mack was right. Those were adolescent kisses. She'd never, until now, had anything to compare them to.

But now she'd been kissed by Mack Griffin. And what a kiss it was. He'd started the same way she had, soft as butterflies. But then he'd parted his lips and kissed her with barely enough pressure to convince her that he'd done it on purpose. Then came the feel of his tongue on her closed lips. A tentative touching that seemed to say "Is this all right? I want to taste you but I'd be sad if I scared you."

It was only after she'd almost unconsciously leaned into Mack and given herself up to his superior strength, expertise and talent, that he actually slid his tongue along her closed lips, urging them open. At the feel of his hot, wet tongue licking her mouth, her insides began to thrum with a sensation that was familiar, yet much stronger, much more intense with Mack. And he'd barely touched her.

As if he'd heard her thought, he caressed the curve
of her shoulders, then let his fingertips graze her collarbone, then down to the beginning swell of her breasts.
The thrumming inside her began to vibrate as he slowly
moved closer to the tips of her breasts. Then his thumbs
touched the sensitized peaks and she drew in a long,
shuddering breath. Her nipples tightened almost pain-
fully, allowing the soft material of her camisole to slip
down to her waist, leaving her breasts bare.

He made an appreciative sound as he bent his head
to kiss her collarbone, the flat area just above the swell
of her breasts, then touched the top of one breast with
his tongue.

She gasped at the fiery wetness on her naked breast.

Then he stopped.

She stood frozen, waiting for a cue from him to
tell her what came next. But he was as still as she, his
breathing hard and fast but steady.

Finally, she met his dark gaze.

"I didn't mean to scare you," he said.

"But you—" She took a breath. "You didn't. I was—"

He hushed her with a fingertip against her lips. "Yes,
I did," he said, taking her hand and holding it up so she
could see it. To her embarrassment, she saw that it was
trembling.

"I guess I'm just tired," she said, persisting in her
pretense that he hadn't startled and frightened her when
he tongued her breast.

He stepped backward and gave her a brief nod. "I
guess," he said.

She felt her face burn. She groped for the straps to
her camisole and started to tug them up. "You think
I'm just a country mouse, don't you, Mr. Hotshot P.I?"

"No," he said with an upturn in his tone that made
his answer sound like a question.

Hannah propped her fists on her hips and glared at him. "Oh, yeah? Then what do you think?"

He assessed her, his eyes still dark with longing. "I think you're a lot more sheltered than you let on."

She bristled, and he held up a hand.

"I'm not saying you're naive. You're not. But you lived an insular life, taking care of your mother, didn't you? Never went out to parties or events. You knew that you needed to be at home for your mom. And your only male role models were the men your mom brought home. Most of them were poorly educated, immature males who thought that their masculinity depended on how well their woman obeyed them."

"Could you stop with the Sherlock Holmes shtick?" Hannah said. His description of her mother, her mother's boyfriends and her cut very close to the bone. And she didn't like it.

"What you've experienced is not what a man is all about. A real man takes care of the woman he loves, sure. But he does it because he respects her, and he treats her with honor. A real man will never hurt a woman. That's the difference between boys and men, Hannah."

Hannah felt as though if she said one more word, she would burst into tears. And there was no way she was going to let Mack Griffin see her shed even one tear now. Not one.

"Come on," Mack said. "Get in bed. I'm going out to have a look around, make sure I don't see our friend or his vehicle out there anywhere, and then I'll be back to tuck you in. How's that?"

Hannah sent him a curious look, wondering if he was using *tuck you in* as a euphemism for sex, but he'd already turned and was slipping his feet into his loafers and grabbing a shirt. "I'll be back in less than ten minutes." He started toward the door, then turned. "Oh, by the way. There's a chance we might have to get out of here in a hurry. Let me have everything but your toothbrush and comb. I'll put them in the car, just in case."

"I'd rather keep my purse," she said, picking it up and hugging it to her chest. When she did, the envelope popped out the top.

"What's that?" Mack asked, eyeing the white envelope.

Hannah pushed it back down into her purse. "Nothing," she said shortly. From the look Mack gave her, she knew she'd answered too quickly and too abruptly, and she knew he wasn't going to let it go. But she hoped he would.

"What's the deal with the envelope, Hannah? I've seen sticking out before," he said, gazing at her steadily with a glint of challenge in his eye. "Does it have something to do with Billy Joe's murder or your mom?"

Hannah's fingers tightened on her purse. "No," she said. "At least—no. Nothing to do with the murder."

"Your mom?"

"Why are you so interested in a silly envelope?"

He shrugged. "Probably because you're so intent on not telling me anything about it. Is it some kind of bad news?"

"Bad news?" she laughed. "Good question. Why don't you read it if you're so curious?"

Mack took the envelope and gave it a cursory glance. "You haven't read it?"

Thoroughly sick of his nosiness, Hannah shook her head in disgust. "No. I haven't. It's from my mother. When she found out she was going to have to go on hemodialysis, she was certain she was on her way out, so she wrote that. She joked that it was her deathbed confession. I told her there was no way I was reading it while she was alive, so that's why she added *in the event of Stephanie Clemens's death* on there."

"Maybe you should read it."

Her eyes widened. "Why? Why do you say that?"

Mack looked at the letter and back up at her. "Just a hunch. Maybe there is something that could help you." He held it out to her.

She took it, then stood there, staring at the writing on the front, then touching it with a fingertip. "Why would you think—" She stopped, lifting her gaze to his. "You know what's in here, don't you?" She waved the envelope at him. "What did you do? You *read* my letter?"

"I just… I saw the envelope and figured there might be something in there that could help your case."

"My case? My *case?*"

"You know what I mean."

Did she?

Hannah looked up. "What?"

"Did your mom ruin your life?"

She shrugged. "I don't know. It was my life, the only one I had. It doesn't feel ruined." She took a deep breath, tore the envelope open and took out the folded piece of paper. "At least it's not a *long* letter," she murmured as she began to read.

"You feel like reading it aloud?" Mack asked.

"Oh, why not. You've already seen it."

"My Darling Hannah,

I've never told you anything about your family. I always told myself that it was for your own good. I think I wanted to believe that, but of course that's not true. I kept it from you because I didn't want to have to answer your questions and listen to you begging me to take you to meet them. But that was selfish of me. You need to know your family and you need to get everything you deserve from them.

My mother, your grandmother, and I have been estranged for years and years. I was born out of wedlock, as they used to say. Mother had me in France. She's never told me who my father is, just as I've never told you who yours is. It strikes me as I write this that I'm a lot more like my mother than I ever thought I was. Surprisingly, I think that makes me happier than sad.

Your grandmother knows about my illness. I wrote her a letter similar to this, which I know she got because I received a handwritten acknowledgment. I actually think it might be nice to see her again, but I doubt I'll have the chance now.

Okay, here goes. The information you need in order to find your grandmother and her family. Your grandmother is Claire Delancey. She is the sister of Robert Connor Delancey, the infamous Louisiana politician. His grandchildren are your cousins.

The Delanceys live in Chef Voleur, Louisiana, on the north shore of Lake Pontchartrain. But I understand that several of your cousins live and work in the city.

I hope you get to meet your grandmother and, if possible, that one day we can see her together. Love,
Your mother."

Hannah folded up the letter and put it back into the envelope, then stuffed the envelope back down into her purse. "Here. You can put my purse in the car," she said.

"What about the letter?"

"What about it? I've never known anything about my mother's family my entire life, so why should I get all excited because she wants to get everything off her chest before she dies?"

"Maybe she wants you to be taken care of."

"And why would a strange family do that?"

"Hannah," Mack said. "I happen to know the Delanceys. They're great people and they've welcomed strangers into their lives and family many times before. Did you recognize Claire's brother's name? You know who Con Delancey is, don't you?"

"I've heard the name. The politician she was talking about?"

Mack nodded. "A wealthy and notorious politician and your grandmother's brother. He might have been governor of the state of Louisiana, if he hadn't been murdered."

"Murdered?" she echoed. "He was murdered?"

"Apparently by his personal assistant, Armand Broussard."

"You know them? The Delanceys?" Hannah said, feeling a sensation in her chest that she barely recognized and didn't like. It was kind of an empty feeling—a lonely feeling. She'd never had siblings or even cousins to play with. Never had a family she could call her own. "How? How do you know them?"

"Well, Dawson, my boss, is a Delancey."

Hannah rubbed her hand just below her collarbone where the lonesome feeling was. "Are you going to tell them?"

He nodded. "I've told Dawson."

"You told him?"

"Sure. He's helping us. I think he deserves to know that he's helping a member of his family, doesn't he?"

"He probably deserves to have a choice as to whether he considers me part of his family."

"Trust me, he's checking you out."

"Oh. Well, that's not going to go in my favor, is it?"

"Don't underestimate him or the rest of the Delanceys."

"They're nice?" she asked. "Have you met my—my grandmother?"

"No, I haven't. But some of the Delanceys think she'll be coming back to Chef Voleur from France."

"Coming back? Really? Why now, after all this time?"

"I think her long-term companion, Ektor Petrakis, just died recently."

For some reason, Hannah felt like crying. Her grandmother might return to the United States. She could get to meet her and maybe, just maybe, her mom could reunite with her mother, too.

But the other side of that daydream was that at any time during the past twenty-six years, either Claire or Hannah's mom could have made the effort to find the other. The odd lonely feeling grew inside her chest again, and she knew it would be only a matter of seconds before the tears started.

"Shouldn't you get that stuff into the car?" she said tightly.

He nodded and grabbed the rest of the items.

She watched him until he closed the motel room door behind him. Then she climbed into bed, curled up on her side and at last, let a few tears fall.

Chapter Eleven

Mack loaded their things into the car, then, after looking around at the parking lot, the cross streets and the other shops in the area, he got in and drove the car around to the back side of the hotel, where the trash bins and air-conditioning units were. Beyond that side of the motel was a large storage rental complex that also held rental trucks and tractor-trailers. The vehicles and the metal storage buildings made a fairly effective fence, hiding the back of the motel. Happy with his decision, he walked back around the side of the motel. As he did, his phone rang.

It was Dawson.

"Hey, man," Mack said. "I was just thinking about you. What did you find out?"

"I had Dusty search through birth records in France. Turns out my computer whiz speaks and writes six languages. She did find the record of birth of a daughter to a Claire Delancey. Judging by the date, that would be Stephanie Martin. Dusty said the last name would be pronounced Mar-tan, being French."

"Wow," Mack said. "So Stephanie would be your first cousin and Hannah is your second cousin."

"Yeah, I guess," Dawson said, sounding a bit as if he was still having trouble believing the relationship.

"Dawson, I know this is going to be hard, but can you keep this quiet? This is going to be huge news for your family, but until we have definitive proof that this woman is really Hannah Martin, I'm thinking it would be better not to upset your family."

"I haven't changed my mind. I agree with you completely. Now, you want to tell me what's going on with this alleged cousin of mine, Hannah Martin?"

"Yeah," Mack said. "It's a long story and it involves drugs and stolen money and murder. I'm going to need your help to get Hannah and her mother out of all this safely."

"Okay," Dawson said on a sigh. "Go ahead. I don't guess I'm going to get to bed within the next hour or two."

Mack took a deep breath and proceeded to give Dawson every bit of information he'd gotten from Hannah as well as everything he'd figured out himself. The only thing he left out was the red tattoo.

Within ten minutes, Mack and Dawson had put together the beginnings of a plan. Dawson would put Dusty to work setting up tracking on the phone of the man who was following Hannah. They had his cell phone information because of the threatening calls he'd made to Hannah. Mack wanted to turn the tables and follow and capture him and find out just how deep Ficone was into drug trafficking in Texas from him.

Dawson had a few suggestions and they argued about a couple of things, but basically, by the time Dawson hung up, Mack was fairly happy with the plan so far.

Hannah spent a couple of minutes in self-indulgent crying, then turned over and lay there, staring into space. The information her mother had given her in the letter was a lot to take in, especially now with everything that was going on. She'd never had many people around her, never really wanted them. But suddenly she was the center of a lot of attention, controversy and drama, and she'd just discovered she was a part of a family she'd never known existed.

Then there was Mack. Her face turned hot against the pillow just thinking about him. Why had she flirted with him? She'd never been a flirt. Years of living with her mom's boyfriends had made her wary of attracting that kind of attention.

So what had possessed her to say even mildly suggestive things to Mack, like *Then I'll take care of you on the floor,* or *That's* Girl Scout *to you, in case you can't tell.*

And then she'd kissed him. She'd surprised herself as much if not more than him. Still, it was his fault. How in the world was she supposed to be so close to him as she tended to his cuts and scrapes and not want to kiss that beautiful, injured face? Being that close to him did things to her insides that she'd never experienced before.

Not that she was entirely innocent. She'd had a couple of boyfriends, the operative word being *boy.* But Mack was definitely no boy. He was a man, through and through. His confident kisses, his gentle, deft touch, assured her of that. He'd showed her a man's desire, and he'd touched and kissed her and tongued her breast to communicate that desire. If he hadn't stopped, what would have happened?

A thrill hummed along her nerve endings and sent her heart racing. Mack would have made love to her. He would have continued kissing and tasting her until she was begging him. Just the thought of him inside her fired her blood in a way she'd never dreamed of. She gasped as her insides throbbed and heat spread through her, all the way to her fingertips.

The sound of a key card in the door startled her. She shifted in the bed so she could see the door as Mack came into the room. He closed the door and for a moment he stood there, the sculpted planes of his face and body outlined by the pale light from the open window. Hannah's breasts tightened just watching him.

After a moment, he pulled the curtains closed, then walked over to the other bed, took off his shoes and lay down, sighing as he did so.

"Mack?" she whispered.

"Yeah?"

"Is everything okay?"

She heard the sheets rustle as he changed position. "Sure."

"Mack?"

This time he didn't answer her.

She swallowed as desire rose inside her. "Would you like to sleep over here?" she asked in a small voice.

He didn't say anything for a long time. Finally, she heard him draw in a long breath. "That's not a good idea," he said softly.

Disappointed and yet in a way relieved, Hannah let out the breath she'd been holding. "I know," she said regretfully. She turned onto her side and tried to ignore the sharp, aching awareness of him lying so close to her. After a few seconds of silence, she swallowed.

"Mack?"

"Yeah, hon?" he muttered.

"It doesn't have to be a good idea."

She heard him sigh, then he was quiet for so long, she thought he might have gone to sleep.

"I don't—" he started, then stopped. "We wouldn't work," he said finally.

She waited, but he didn't say anything else. She turned over onto her back and stared at the ceiling, where the light from the motel's parking lot made odd shadows. "I don't understand."

"I'd break your heart."

She glanced over at him. She could see his profile outlined by the pale light. "Really?" she said. "You think I'm that weak? You think you need to protect me from *you* because I can't take care of myself?"

He didn't answer.

"You do! You think I'm like my mom. You think I have no judgment when it comes to men." She paused, trying to control her anger.

"I think you've learned all the wrong things," he said. "Your mom is an alcoholic and you've been exposed to too much of the bad side of relationships. But I've seen even worse, been through worse."

"Worse?" Hannah said on a short laugh, thinking if that was true then what he'd seen had to be horrific. "You've been through worse than cleaning up after your mom's drunken binges? Worse than watching her get hit by her boyfriends? Worse than dodging their fists yourself?"

"I watched a man kill my mom when I was twelve."

Hannah gasped. "Oh, Mack—" she said, her voice breaking.

"Don't," he snapped. "I just wanted to warn you. I don't do relationships."

Hannah's mouth twisted into a wry smile. "I didn't ask you to marry me, just to—"

"Hannah, don't put yourself in that position," he said tersely, then turned onto his side, away from her. She

listened to his breathing as it settled, slowed down and
became more even. She concentrated on its rhythm,
using it to temper her own breathing and pulse. With
great deliberation, she kept her mind on his and her
breathing and refused to allow any other thoughts in.
Eventually, Mack's breathing changed. He was asleep.

Still matching her breathing to his, Hannah finally
felt herself relax. She filled her inner vision with the
image of him standing in the bathroom door in nothing
but pajama pants, his skin sparkling with water droplets.
It was a dangerous thing to do, to dream about Mack.

He'd made himself perfectly clear. He didn't do relationships. She believed him, because she'd seen the
hard glint in his eyes and the stubborn angle of his jaw.
He meant what he said.

That side of him broke her heart, though, because
she'd seen the other side—the sweet, vulnerable side
that he did his best to keep hidden. She knew that side
would always lose out to the other, stronger side that
he'd developed to protect himself.

If she could turn back time and go back to before any
of the awful events that had filled up the past days had
happened, would she? No. She knew she'd never choose
to go back to the time before she'd known Mack. No matter what happened in the future, for tonight, she had him.
For the first time, she realized she was becoming truly
relaxed. As she began to drift into sleep, her last thought
was that she could sleep, because Mack was there with
her, his strong, warm body protecting her from danger.

THE MAN WITH *the red tattoo raised his gun and shot,
and Billy Joe fell right where he stood. But the man
kept shooting and Billy Joe kept falling—*

Hannah was halfway out of the bed before she fully

woke up. Her throat constricted as a scream tried to push its way out.

Mack was already up and at the window, his hand pushing the curtains aside. "It's okay," he said, peering out. "Bunch of drunks."

The scream still clawed at her throat, thrumming in the same staccato rhythm as her racing pulse. She couldn't get a full breath.

Outside their door, the noise sorted itself into fists banging on a door, shouts of "Open up, we've got beer," and from farther away, "Shut up or I'll call the police" and "I'm calling the manager."

Mack checked the locks, glanced through the curtains once more as the commotion began to wind down, then crossed the room to her. He touched her chin, coaxing her to raise her head. "Hey, Hannah," he said softly. "Are you okay?"

She shuddered as her heart began to slow down and her muscles relaxed. She took a deep breath, finally. "The man with the red tattoo was shooting Billy Joe," she muttered. "He wouldn't stop shooting."

"Okay," Mack said. He slid an arm around her waist and guided her toward her bed. "Sit down. I'll get you some water. Don't think about what you were dreaming."

Hannah sat, doing her best to relax. She felt as though her muscles were still tied in knots. When Mack brought her a glass of water, she drank it all. He set the glass on the bedside table, then sat beside her.

"How're you doing now?"

Outside, a couple of guys were still talking loudly. Then a door slammed and like an echo, two doors farther away slammed, as well. "I guess the excitement is over," she said shakily. To her dismay, as she relaxed, reaction set in and she began to tremble.

"Oh, no." Her eyes stung and a trio of little sobs escaped.

Mack put his arm around her and pulled her close. He kissed the top of her head. She slid an arm around his waist, her hand sliding across his taut back muscles and savoring the heat of his body. He straightened.

"I'll get you some more water," he said.

"No, please," she responded, pulling him closer. "Just stay here."

But he stood and she had to let go. He walked back over to the other bed. She followed him and caught his hand. When he turned toward her, his mouth set, his eyes hard, she wrapped her hand around his neck, stood on tiptoe and kissed him.

"Stop it," he muttered, but she ignored him. She let her tongue flirt gently with his closed lips, and smiled when she felt him begin to respond.

Mack couldn't stop his body from reacting to Hannah's kiss. He'd never gotten this close to anyone like her—never allowed himself to. She packed a lethal combination of innocence, sexuality and vulnerability that he instinctively avoided—normally. Although he couldn't remember ever having this much trouble resisting. It was all about proximity, he figured. He'd always been a master at steering clear of women like her.

But Hannah's mouth was so soft and sexy as her tongue played with his in an erotic dance that nearly pushed him over the edge. He was hard and growing harder, and he had to stop her before it was too late.

He pulled away, then pressed his forehead to hers and closed his eyes. "Hannah. This is such a bad idea. Don't make me reject you. Don't make me hurt you."

She lifted her head just enough to touch her lips to his. "You think I don't have a mind of my own?" she whispered, kissing him softly again. "Do you actually think you're the one in control here?"

He felt her mouth widen in a smile, then she slid her tongue across his lips. "You're in for a big surprise, mister."

He wrapped his arms around her and pulled her to him, turning her teasing kiss into the erotic dance she'd started earlier. "Don't make this more than it is," he muttered as he slid his hands down to her breasts and lower to catch the hem of her pajama top and pull it off over her head.

Hannah lifted her arms, then wrapped them around his neck and kissed him more deeply yet. She took his hand and placed it on her bare breast. Then she slid his pajama bottoms down and caressed his buttocks. "Come to bed," she whispered, pulling him with her as she lay down.

Then they were together, wound around each other. Mack was inside her and somehow, he had the feeling she was inside him. He'd never felt like this before. As if he'd finally found the missing part of himself. When he could no longer hold back, he sank himself deeply into her and heard her breath catch. He thrust again and again, until he felt her contracting around him, then his own climax overwhelmed him.

When the sensations finally waned and he lay with his head resting on her shoulder, he struggled to stay in the fantasy the two of them had created. But he couldn't. As he drifted off to sleep, a single rational thought pushed its way into his mind.

He was so screwed.

MACK WOKE UP when the sky began to lighten, around six o'clock. Right away, he was aware of Hannah asleep next to him. Hell, who was he kidding. He'd been aware of her all night. He'd woken a couple of times with hunger gnawing at his insides and arousal aching in his groin.

He held his breath for a couple of seconds and listened to her soft, even breaths. He was glad she was sleeping soundly. She'd been hysterical the night before, when those drunken idiots had banged on the door. He'd been scared, too. After all, there was a high probability that the man with the red tattoo would find them. But Mack was betting his own odds that the guy wouldn't want to fight him again. Certainly not by himself.

Once the drunks were gone, Hannah had flung herself at him, crying, her whole body trembling. He'd gathered her into his arms and held her, comforting her and reminding her that he was here, between her and the door, and that he'd keep her safe, no matter what.

Then he'd made a fatal mistake. He'd allowed himself to consider the possibility of making love to her. He'd quickly tried to banish the thought from his head, but it had been too late.

Hannah's crying had calmed, and her desperately tight hug had relaxed. He'd felt the supple changes in her body and face that indicated sexual arousal. She'd kissed him, not softly, not sweetly. No, her kiss had been hungry, passionate, demanding. In the soft, quiet darkness, Mack had surrendered and made love with her.

And now, this morning, regret weighed him down like a dozen anvils on his chest. He'd known in the back of his mind that this would happen. He'd tried to tell her. But she'd been too desirable and he'd been too weak to resist her.

He couldn't remember when touching a woman had

been so exciting and new. Or when he'd ever given up so much of himself to any woman. He'd had a lot of sex, but he felt as though last night was the first time he'd ever really *made love* with a woman.

And now, because his lust had overridden his ingrained caution regarding a woman like Hannah, who needed his protection, Mack had put himself in an impossible position.

There was only one way he could effectively protect her. By locking away his desire for her the same way he'd learned to lock away physical and emotional pain. As long as he kept his personal feelings separate from his self-imposed responsibility for her, he could keep her safe—he hoped.

For a while, Mack lay still, listening to Hannah's soft, even breaths. He had a plan, as far as it went. Most of what he'd done since she'd knocked on his door had been based purely on instinct. That wasn't his way. He'd never been good at going by the book, but he did have his own rules. And Rule #1 in the MacEllis Griffin Operations Handbook was "Always Have a Plan."

He threw back the covers and got up, carefully washed his bandaged face and brushed his teeth. Then he quietly dressed, stuck his wallet and his car keys into his pockets, grabbed the motel room key and slipped out the door and into the coolness of early morning, hoping he hadn't woken Hannah. Taking deep breaths of the pleasantly fresh air, Mack thought about the past three days. *Three days.* Had he only known Hannah for three days? It seemed as if she'd been with him for years.

After a short walk that made him feel a lot better, Mack went into the small front desk area of the motel to check out the continental breakfast they advertised. All he saw was a pot of coffee, a pitcher of orange juice and some rather stale-looking muffins on a tray. He downed a glass of orange juice, then poured two cups of coffee and put them and two of the muffins on a plastic carrying tray. He started toward the double glass doors to head back to their room, when he saw the early-morning sun's reflection on a big maroon sedan that was turning into the parking lot.

Reflexively, he glanced at his watch. Six-thirty. Then he took another quick look at the car. It was definitely maroon, and it looked familiar. His pulse hammered in his ears as he squinted, trying to get a glimpse of the driver.

As the car headed straight for the front desk of the motel, right where he was standing, he finally saw the driver. He was big and bald, with biceps bulging from a dark T-shirt. It had to be him. The man with the red tattoo. So he'd found them. That actually fit in with what he and Dawson had talked about, but if Mack was going to turn the tables on the man, he had to keep himself and Hannah alive long enough to do it.

MACK SET THE tray down on one of the tables. He stepped up to the front desk, but no one was there. He rang the bell furiously.

A woman with what appeared to be a permanent scowl came out of the back room. "Yeah?" she said grudgingly.

"Is there a back way out of here?" he asked quickly.

"What for?" she muttered, her keen, black eyes giving him a suspicious look.

He gave her a sheepish shrug. "See that maroon car? That's the husband of the woman I'm here with."

She gave Mack a world-weary look. "Like I never heard—"

"Please," he begged. "We were high school sweethearts."

She jerked a thumb toward her shoulder. "Through that door. Y'all get in a fight and I'll call the cops on you."

Mack winked at her. "We're already gone," he said.

Heading out the back of the motel, Mack breathed a sigh of relief. When he looked down the rear of the rows of rooms, he saw the Beemer and felt the tightness in his chest loosen. Thank goodness he'd parked the car around back last night.

Now if he could just get Hannah out of the room safely, they'd be in good shape. They might even be able to get ahead of the maroon car so they could get to Dowdie and get set up for the rest of the plan, which hadn't been completely worked out yet.

Mack pulled out his phone and speed-dialed Hannah's number, but she didn't answer. "Still asleep?" he muttered to himself as he dialed again.

"Come on," he whispered. "Hannah, come on. Where are you?"

He found the nearest breezeway that led from the back of the motel to the front and crept to the corner, trying to peer around without being seen. There, to his left, he saw the maroon car. The man had backed it into a parking space across from the motel entrance and was idling.

What the hell was he doing? Then he saw Hannah, dressed in shorts, a T-shirt and tennis shoes, walking toward the front desk. She'd already passed the breezeway where he was hiding.

Mack ran down to the next breezeway. He had to get

Hannah's attention, intercept her and head for the car before the guy made his move to grab her.

As Hannah approached, Mack called out in a stage whisper, "Hannah, over here."

She stopped and looked around.

"Keep walking. It's me, Mack. Don't look around."

She turned her head toward the sound of his voice. "Mack?" she whispered.

"Don't talk. Just walk," he whispered. "When you get to the breezeway—" An engine revved and the maroon car pulled out of its parking space. The transmission squealed as the driver slammed it into First and floored it.

"Run!" Mack shouted to Hannah.

She ran toward the breezeway.

"Run!" he shouted again. "I'm getting the car!"

Hannah had no idea what was going on and no time to think. She heard a car behind her, approaching way too fast. She ran as fast as she could. As she reached the breezeway, tires screeched as the car took the corner into the breezeway and hit the left concrete wall. Pieces of metal and glass flew everywhere.

Broken safety glass peppered Hannah's skin but she couldn't stop. Mack had sounded nearly panicked.

She pumped her legs harder and gasped for air. Then over the noise of the car's engine and her own footsteps crunching on the asphalt, she heard a more ominous sound. It was the slamming of a car door.

Suddenly, she was thrown into déjà vu. The man was going to shoot her. She knew it. She doubted she'd be so lucky as to dodge his bullets for a second time.

Then she saw the white BMW pull up to the end of the breezeway and stop. *Mack.* She forced her aching legs to push harder, forced herself not to think about her spasming, oxygen-starved lungs or the bullet that could stop her at any second.

Behind her, she heard the unmistakable sound of a gunshot. Her muscles contracted automatically and she almost lost her footing. The bullet hit the wall beside her head with a thunk, then zinged past her. Or was that a second bullet?

In front of her, Mack flung the BMW's passenger door open. For Hannah, the next few seconds went by in slow motion. She felt the impact through her whole body as her right foot came down on the asphalt. Then her left foot hit the hard ground. She concentrated on going as fast as she could, no matter how jarring each stride was.

Two sharp reports sounded behind her and her neck muscles tightened, sending pain up through the top of her head.

That had been too close. In front of her, from the shadow of the car's interior, Mack was yelling something, but all she could hear was the zing of bullets echoing in her ears. A deep dent appeared in the white-painted metal of the BMW as if by magic, and in the next instant, Hannah felt a searing heat on the inside of her right elbow.

She had to slow down. *Had to.* Not only because she had no more breath, but also because if she didn't, she'd hurtle through the open passenger door of the Beemer with no control and dive headfirst into Mack, who was revving the engine in preparation for speeding away as soon as she was inside the car.

As she slowed, her perception of time sped up, so that by the time she hit the leather passenger seat of the white car, she was able to grab the door frames, lessening her impact on Mack by forcing her arms to take the recoil.

The next thing she knew, she was right side up, sitting in the leather bucket seat, heaving uncontrollably as Mack burned rubber getting out of the motel parking lot.

Mack drove silently, intensely, until he got onto the interstate and managed to put fifteen minutes between them and the motel. Hannah spent the time regaining control of her breathing and checking behind them for any sign of the maroon car. After a couple of minutes, she sat with her head back against the headrest and her eyes closed, trying not to think about anything. Trying merely to be grateful she was alive and grateful that she hadn't tripped or miscalculated and run into the Beemer's door instead of managing to aim correctly for the opening into the car.

Finally, after a long time, Hannah said, "Mack, he's probably tracking us through my phone. Can't people do that these days? I should turn it off."

"That's exactly right," Mack said. "He is tracking us through your phone. But actually, we're tracking him, too."

"We're what? How?"

"Dawson got his computer whiz to set it up. Piece of cake, since the guy called you twice."

"Called me twice? How do you know that?"

"You left your access code to your voice mail set at the default. The last four digits of your telephone number. Anybody could get in."

"You listened to my voice mail?" She frowned, thinking of Billy Joe's telephone tirades. She felt her face grow hot. "I can't believe you did that."

Mack shook his head. "I could have gotten the transcripts from the Metairie Police. Same difference."

She huffed and crossed her arms, turning away to look out the passenger-side window. "Well, then, you should have. A person's phone messages are private."

Mack laughed. "Not really. Not these days."

For a moment, both of them were silent, but Hannah wanted to hear what Dawson and his computer person were doing with the man's phone. "Okay, fine. So what's happening with tracking the man?"

"Dawson's getting the info from Dusty and texting me his position," Mack said. "By the way, the man's name is Hoyt Diller."

Hannah heard a hard, brittle tone in Mack's voice, but within a couple of seconds, he reached over and squeezed her hand briefly. "We've turned the tables on him and we're leading him to Dowdie, hopefully to trap him and, if we're lucky, Ficone. But we've had to bring in the sheriff. We need him and his deputies to help us. There's no way we can handle this ourselves."

"The sheriff? But won't he arrest me? I mean, not only am I accused of drugs and maybe murder, I also fled the jurisdiction, right?"

Mack nodded. "Since we both swore in writing that you wouldn't leave the jurisdiction while out on bail, you're in violation of a court order, at the least. At worst, there will be a warrant out for your arrest. I could be brought before the bar, but I'm not too worried about that. I was planning to let my license to practice lapse anyhow."

Hannah took a deep breath. "So what now?"

"I'd like to think that the desk clerk heard the gunshots and called the cops, but even if she did, there's a good chance they're just now getting there."

"Do you think the cops will arrest him?"

Mack took out his phone and glanced at the screen. "Looks like he's back on the road, about twenty minutes behind us."

Hannah looked in the passenger-side mirror again, then turned around to get a good look. "I don't see him," she said. "That's good, right?"

"Yeah, for what it's worth. We're on U.S. 49. It's a pretty good road."

Mack looked up at the stretch of road in front of him, then glanced in his rearview mirror. "I'd rather be on the narrow county roads. That car he's driving is awfully low to the ground. A couple of good bumps and he'll knock a hole in the radiator and be stuck on the road while we just drive right on into Dowdie."

"This car is too low, too," she pointed out.

"The shocks are probably four times as good as his car."

Hannah shook her head. "The chassis is too low. It'll be as bad as the maroon car, trying to drive fast on those rough roads. We need a pickup."

Mack considered their options. There weren't many. "Okay, then," he said, looking around him at the town they were passing through. "Look. There's a used-car dealership up ahead. Let's trade the Beemer for a pickup."

Chapter Twelve

It was after nine o'clock at night when Hannah drove the teal-blue Ford pickup into Dowdie and turned onto the road to her mother's house. "The house is about two miles down this road," she said.

"I see what you mean about your neighbors."

"The closest one is Mr. Jones, about a mile away. But out here, there's not much light pollution, so you can see car lights or a porch light from a long way away.

"We have forty acres. Mom didn't realize the place was that big when she bought it ten years ago. The house is on the center lot, so we have plenty of room on either side. And with those tall spruces that line the road as a windbreak, you can't really see the house or much of the garage from the road."

"It's a two-car garage, right?"

"Yeah," she said. "But Billy Joe's Mustang takes up one whole side, and his tools and equipment take up the other. It'll probably take us all night to move his tools and equipment so we can hide the pickup in there."

"I'll take care of that while you make sure we can stay in the house without anyone knowing we're there. And think about where Billy Joe hid the money."

"And where my mother is."

Mack nodded grimly and Hannah knew what he was

thinking as clearly as if he'd said it aloud. Mack didn't think her mother was still alive. With Billy Joe dead, she'd probably been tied up or confined for two days without food or water.

"Here's the house, on the right."

"I can see why Billy Joe liked this place."

Hannah nodded. "It was perfect for him. I don't think he ever cared for my mom. I think he saw our place and it was just gravy that a single woman owned it. He wasn't happy to have me around, but he had to put up with me to get all this." She'd shut off the truck's headlights before she'd turned onto their road. She pulled into their driveway and drove around behind the garage so the truck couldn't be easily seen from the road.

"Where's Hoyt?"

Mack checked. "We made lots better time in the pickup than he is. He's about two hours behind us and—" he paused as a buzz announced another text "—hah. He's turned and headed south. He's going to Galveston, I'll bet. Maybe he'll bring Ficone back here."

"You're happy about that?"

"It falls in with our plan. We're hoping not only to catch Hoyt, but Sal Ficone, a pretty big drug dealer on the Gulf Coast."

She nodded. "I think we can safely stay in the basement without being seen," she told Mack as she shut off the engine. "The sliding glass doors face the woods. Mom put up blackout curtains to keep the sun off the patio. The whole front of the house is open, though. You can see into the living room and dining room at night. We won't be able to go upstairs for anything." She climbed out of the driver's side of the truck as Mack got out of the passenger seat.

"Then the basement it is. Can you fix us up places to sleep?"

Hannah nodded. "There's a couch down there that opens into a double bed. It's kind of old but it's not too uncomfortable."

"Okay, why don't you head on inside. I'm going to start on the garage."

"Do you want something to eat?" she asked.

"Damn it," Mack said. "I meant to stop and get us something."

"There's a freezer full of food in the basement. We'll be fine."

He nodded. "I'm starving. Is there something easy you can fix for tonight? What time is it?"

"It's kind of late. After ten."

Mack studied her. "You're exhausted. Forget food. I'll find us something, even if it's crackers and coffee."

"Don't worry about me. I've been more tired than this. Earlier this week." She smiled shyly. "I feel pretty good now."

Mack winced at the implication. She was referring to their lovemaking the night before. He had been doing his best to put it out of his mind. It was a sign of his weakness that he'd given in to his desires and made love with her. It didn't matter that it was the best thing, the most wonderful thing, he'd ever experienced. He'd compromised her safety by allowing himself to get involved with her.

"It's no problem making you some dinner," Hannah continued.

As she spoke, Mack's phone rang. He looked at the display. It was Dawson. "It's Dawson. I need to talk to him. I'll be inside in a few minutes."

"Come around the back and through the basement

door. Watch your step. The sidewalk going down the hill is cracked. You could trip."

Mack watched Hannah navigate the old sidewalk and then answered the phone. "Dawson?"

"Mack, we found Stephanie Clemens."

"Found her? Is she all right?" Mack asked, hardly breathing.

"She's alive. She's dehydrated and in shock. But she's being rushed to Dallas for emergency hemodialysis and the doctors are optimistic."

Mack was relieved, for Hannah's sake. "Good," he said. "Where'd you find her?"

"In an apartment just outside of Paris, Texas, that was rented to Campbell. About the time we tracked it down, the police received a call complaining that loud music had been playing for three days. They found her locked in the bathroom. She'd gone into liver failure so she was unconscious. The paramedics said she'd probably been out no more than six hours."

"And what hospital is she going to?" Mack asked.

Dawson told him.

"Thanks, Dawson. If her mother dies, I'm not sure Hannah could stand it."

"Trust me, Mack. I understand. Now listen, since Hoyt has turned south, you've got overnight to be ready for them. We have no idea exactly what time they might be there tomorrow, or even if they'll make it back to Dowdie that soon, but at least you can be ready. I've already talked to the sheriff."

Mack and Dawson briefly discussed the rest of the plan, then Dawson hung up and Mack ducked under the crime-scene tape crisscrossed over both the overhead garage door and the side door.

When he turned the knob on the door, it opened and

he stepped inside. Pulling a small, high-powered flashlight out of his pocket, he shone it around.

On the other side of the garage, he saw the distinctive shape of a vintage Mustang Cobra. He looked at the polished red finish, the chrome cobra on the side along with the letters *SVT*. Hannah had mentioned that Billy Joe had a Mustang, but she hadn't told him it was a *Special Vehicle Team* Cobra.

"Nice," he muttered as he examined the car. It was in beautiful condition. As the flashlight's beam played over the shiny surface from the rear to the front, he saw that the hood had been removed, leaving the engine exposed.

From what Mack could tell, and he certainly knew very little about working on cars, the engine was partially disassembled. A soft blanket was thrown over the car's fender to protect the paint job from scratches.

Mack turned his attention to the rest of the garage. As Hannah had said, there were tools and supplies everywhere, and right inside the side door was a wooden workbench that stuck out about four feet from the far wall. If he moved the workbench, rolled a couple of car-lifts over in front of the Mustang, then picked up empty parts boxes and toolboxes and moved two large trash cans outside, the truck would fit easily.

It took him about forty minutes to take care of everything. Finally, he was able to open the garage door, ripping the crime-scene tape to shreds in the process, and drive the truck into the garage in the dark. It fit almost perfectly. With a sigh of relief, he closed the garage door with a passing glance at the ruined crime-scene tape, closed the side door, then headed down the sidewalk to the basement and slipped in through the sliding glass doors.

Inside, Hannah had turned on a lamp, which lent a dim glow to the room. Hannah had already folded out the couch into a double bed and made it up with crisp white sheets. The mattress looked droopy but serviceable.

"Mack?" Hannah called. "I'm in here."

He followed her voice through the closest of two doors on either end of the wall behind the couch. The room was a laundry room with a washer, dryer, sink and a small chest freezer. On top of the dryer sat a microwave and a coffeepot. The air held the delicious smell of fresh coffee.

"I got those from upstairs," Hannah said. "I think I've fixed us a pretty good setup here. Want some coffee?"

He nodded gratefully. "But first, is there a bathroom down here?" he asked as she handed him a mug. "I want a shower more than coffee."

"I understand." Hannah nodded toward the interior wall of the laundry room. "It's right there on the other side of that wall. Go ahead. I'm about to dig in the freezer and see what we've got for dinner. I'm thinking it's going to be pizza."

"Works for me," Mack said. He took his plastic bag of clothes into the bathroom with him. The bathroom was large and had a window that opened out onto the side of the house. Rather than take a chance of somebody seeing the light and investigating, Mack hung a towel over the curtain rod.

While Mack showered, Hannah found two frozen microwavable pepperoni pizzas, a package of frozen chopped green peppers and onions and a bag of Italian-style cheese, so she embellished the plain pizzas, then cooked them according to the microwave directions. They wouldn't taste as good out of the microwave as if she'd baked them in an oven, but they would definitely be filling and more nutritious than coffee alone.

She'd taken the first pizza out of the microwave and was inserting the second when Mack came out of the bathroom. She looked up and the sight of him made her knees weak and her mouth dry. He had on jeans with no shirt. He'd flung his wet towel around his neck. His hair was dripping wet and every so often a drop would slither down his cheek or get caught in his long dark eyelashes.

Hannah swallowed a gasp at the sheer beauty of his body.

He met her gaze and sent her a mocking smile, as if he knew and was amused by what she was thinking.

She moistened her lips with her tongue. "Did you have a good shower? Plenty of hot water?" None of that was what she'd wanted to say. She'd wanted to say *You are the most beautiful man I've ever seen.* Instead, she turned away from the enticing sight of his bare shoulders, his lean, hard abs and the jeans riding low on his hips. That wasn't what she'd wanted to do, either. She wanted to forget about food, sleep and danger and bury herself in his hot, hard body. Lose herself in the pleasure he roused in her.

But the things she wanted were not practical, probably not even possible. So she took a deep breath and sent up a brief prayer that Mack couldn't read her mind. "The pizzas are ready," she said, feeling self-conscious. "Are you hungry?"

Mack's hooded, smoky eyes were watching her. They didn't waver when a droplet of water slid over his brow and balanced, shimmering, on his ridiculously long lashes. Finally, he blinked and the droplet and the smokiness disappeared.

In the next second, Hannah couldn't be sure if any of that had happened or if she'd imagined it.

"Hungry?" he said quietly, putting all sorts of meanings into the word. "Yeah, I am."

Doing her best to pretend that his answer was not a double entendre, Hannah handed him a plate filled with slices of pizza and pointed to the living room. "Sit on the end of the bed. Use the coffee table. And if you want, turn on the TV and we can see what the local news has to say about Billy Joe's death." By the time Hannah had brought her plateful of pizza and cup of coffee to the couch, he'd found a network channel that was showing local news. He had closed captioning on and the sound turned low.

They ate in silence and listened as the reporter listed community events and praised the football team. Finally, he turned the camera over to a second reporter.

"Thanks, John. We've been following an incredible story of a local resident, Stephanie Clemens, of Dowdie, who has been missing for several days. Ms. Clemens is a hemodialysis patient and according to her physician's office, as of this morning, she has missed one of her lifesaving treatments. Sheriff Harlan King told our reporter that he's mounting a countywide search for her and her daughter, Hannah Martin, whom he's seeking for questioning in the murder of Billy Joe Campbell, Ms. Clemens's boyfriend. The sheriff has asked that anyone with information regarding the murder of Mr. Campbell or the whereabouts of Ms. Clemens or Ms. Martin call the sheriff's office immediately. Back to you, John."

Mack turned off the TV. "Someone might hear it," he said around his last mouthful of pizza.

"The sheriff is going to mount a search," Hannah said. "You know the first place they'll look is here. Even if we leave, they'll know we've been here. What are we going to do?"

While Mack took their paper plates into the laundry room and threw them into the wastebasket, he debated how much to tell Hannah about what he and Dawson were planning. "I don't think the sheriff is our enemy," he said carefully.

"Maybe he's not, but if he finds me, he's going to arrest me."

"That might not be such a bad idea."

Hannah's mouth dropped open. "What?" She crossed her arms and began pacing back and forth in front of the glass doors with the blackout curtains. "That's not funny."

"Wasn't meant to be."

Disbelief and hurt crossed her face and she wrapped her arms around herself, as if to protect her heart.

"I'm worried about you. I need to know that you're safe."

"Well, I need to know that my mother is safe. Only she's not. She's out there somewhere, sick. Close to dying."

Mack couldn't hold her gaze. He got it. Hannah was terrified for her mother. And as long as her mother was missing, Hannah would never give up. She'd never put her safety ahead of her mom's. He wished he could tell her that her mom had been found and was safe and sound in a Dallas hospital.

But Dawson had provided the voice of reason and

Mack had to agree with him. If Hannah knew her mother had been found and was in the hospital, she'd fight him until he let her go to her. And that was too dangerous.

"Hannah, all I can tell you is that I'm very sure your mom will be all right. What I'm trying to do is stop Ficone and his hired hit man from grabbing you. You do understand that these people are ruthless, don't you? They won't stop until you tell them where their money and drugs are."

"But I can't. I don't *know* where they are."

Mack spread his hands. "*I don't know* is not an acceptable answer to a man like Ficone. Didn't you tell me the man told Billy Joe that Ficone was meeting with his suppliers in three days? That was today. That means if Ficone isn't dead, he's desperate. He's being squeezed from both sides. That makes him dangerous, but I'm betting it will also make him careless. It should be easy to take him and his goon down."

Mack saw in Hannah's face that she'd already moved on to the next logical conclusion. He set his jaw.

"Oh, my God! That's what you're doing. You're not concerned about me or my mother. You're not even interested in stopping Ficone. All you want is revenge for the man you think killed your mother."

"Hannah—"

She laughed, a harsh sound without amusement. "This is great. I'm such an idiot. Of course it's about the man with the red tattoo."

"It's not. You need to listen—"

"I don't need to do anything," she said, swiping her hand through the air in a dismissive gesture. "Don't talk to me unless you're ready to respect me enough to stop lying to me. For someone who demands the truth from others, you sure don't reveal much."

He gave her an ironic smile. "Then we make quite a pair, don't we?" he said.

Chapter Thirteen

Mack took a walk around the house to be sure the basement lights couldn't be seen and that no one was hanging around, he told Hannah. But when he got outside and far enough away that she couldn't hear him, he called Dawson.

"Do you know what time it is?" Dawson asked when he picked up the phone.

"I always know what time it is. Have you talked to the sheriff?" he asked.

There was an infinitesimal pause before Dawson answered. "I have. I've talked to the FBI, too. We're going to have to discuss a few changes. I was going to call you around 5:00 a.m."

Mack frowned. "What kind of changes?"

"I know you want Hannah out of harm's way. But think about this. What if she's there, just like Ficone's man expects? And she shows him that she's looking for the key—the answer to where Billy Joe hid the drugs and money."

"You want to use her for *bait?*" Mack interrupted. "Oh, hell, no."

"Listen, Mack. She'll be safe. You'll have the sheriff and his deputies all around. You'll take them down before they can do anything."

"I said no. What happened to the FBI?"

"They're out now that Ms. Clemens has been found. They were always in it just for the kidnapping."

"Listen to me, Daw. We are *not* putting Hannah in more danger. She's not an agent. She has no idea how to handle herself in a life-or-death situation. Use me. They can question me. I can be the one who figured out what Billy Joe was talking about."

"Come on, Mack. You know that won't work. They'll never believe you. It's got to be Hannah. I'm guessing he hasn't called her again."

"Nope."

"All right. Like we said earlier, we're going on the assumption that they'll be at the house early in the morning. I figure Ficone will probably send two men at least, but you'll have four."

Mack argued with Dawson for a while longer, but he knew he was already defeated. No matter how much he didn't like it, he knew that Dawson's plan was a good one—as long as the bad guys did what they were expected to do.

When Mack got back inside, Hannah had changed into pajamas with a robe that looked like a kimono and he could tell that she was still angry about his idea of letting the sheriff put her in jail.

"Well?" she said.

"What?" He looked at her sharply. Had she seen him talking on his phone? Worse, had she heard him?

"Did you see anything?" she asked. "Wasn't that why you went out?"

"Everything was quiet and dark. No traffic. But you were right. You can see headlights or even a lightbulb from a very long way away." He paused, looking at her. "Why don't you get some sleep? We're going to be up and getting ready by six o'clock. Take the couch. I'm going to keep an eye out."

"Or you could call the sheriff and he could stick me in the *tank*. That'll give you plenty of time to get a good night's sleep without having to worry about me."

"Trust me, I'm tempted," he said wryly. "But Dawson and I talked again and we've given up the idea of locking you up. Too much trouble."

She raised her brows. "Really? I'm thinking I might like this Dawson."

"I made the decision. I decided I want you where I can keep an eye on you. Want more coffee?" he asked casually.

She followed him. "Mack, what's really going on here?"

He sighed. "Nothing's going on. I'm just trying to figure out the best way to handle Ficone."

"No. It's something."

"It's nothing you need to be concerned about." He walked over to the bed and sat down on it, leaning back against the pillows.

"It's about the man with the red tattoo, isn't it?"

Mack sipped his coffee, feeling Hannah watching him. He kept his eyes on the coffee's liquid surface, studying it as intently as if it were tea leaves that might reveal the future.

"Tell me about the tattoo. Ever since I first mentioned it, I've felt like we're headed for some big *High Noon* shootout between you and that murderer. You knew exactly what it looked like. You've seen it before. Talk to me about it. It's obviously eating you up inside."

"I—" He stopped. He'd never talked about what he'd seen. Not to the police when he'd called to tell them his mother was dead. Not even to Dawson. The most he'd ever said about it was to her when he'd told her he'd watched a man kill his mother.

"Oh, Mack," Hannah said, touching his arm with her fingers. "Is this about your mother?"

He closed his eyes for a second, then went back to staring into the coffee cup. "The first time I remember seeing my mother hurt and bloody was when I was about six. I don't remember what the man looked like who hit her. All I remember is that I tried to hit him and he just tossed me aside."

Hannah's fingers tightened on his arm. He thought she was going to say something, but she didn't.

He swirled the coffee around in the bottom of the cup. "It happened at least one more time, with a different boyfriend." He looked up at her, then back at the cup. "I think she actually got one guy put in jail for assault. Then years later, I came home from school one day to find her new boyfriend, a big man with a receding hairline, yelling at her, 'Didn't I tell you not to wake me up with that damned vacuum cleaner?' He yelled, then he hit her with his fist."

Mack stopped, feeling his stomach churn with nausea. He remembered now why he'd never talked about it. Every time the memories tried to push their way into his conscious mind, they made him physically ill and stripped him of his confidence and control, so he shoved it as far to the back of his mind as he could.

His eyes began to sting. He rubbed them with his finger and thumb and noticed that they were damp. He cleared his throat. "Then he picked her—up off the floor and kept on—" He swallowed and cleared his throat again. "I tried to stop him. I was twelve and I was sure I could beat him up."

Hannah made a choked noise and when Mack looked at her, tears were gathering in her eyes.

"I couldn't protect her. I couldn't save her," he said, then shrugged.

"Oh, Mack, you were a child. Of course you couldn't."

He got up and took the cup into the laundry room. Hannah followed him.

"Come on, Hannah. You asked. I told you. Now drop it."

"Mack. You do realize that you couldn't possibly have stopped him, right?"

He turned to her, his jaw tight. "I don't need pop psychology, Hannah. I know all about it. Just drop it," he grated. "I'm not talking any more about it."

Hannah's heart was breaking. She knew what he had gone through. She'd seen the same pattern with her own mother, and she'd sworn to herself that she'd live alone rather than allow a man to treat her that way. No wonder Mack shied away from relationships. No wonder he did his best not to get involved.

She lifted her arms toward him, but he just glared at her and walked away.

"Mack, damn it." She stomped around and stood in front of him just as he was about to unlock the sliding glass doors. "Stop being so stubborn. I just want to hold you."

At that instant, everything about him changed, so suddenly and completely that she was shocked. He gave her a steady, emotionless look like nothing she'd seen from him before, not even when he'd opened his apartment door and seen her standing there. His expression then had shown his irritation at being interrupted. But this—this was as if a machine with a human mask for a face were looking at her. She took an involuntary step backward and lowered her arms.

"I told you, Hannah. I suck at relationships. I usually date women who don't want one. It works out well for both of us."

"You don't mean that. You're the strongest yet most gentle man I've ever known," she said. "You are—"

Before she could even finish her sentence, he turned on his heel, opened the sliding door and left.

Hannah stared after him for a long time. Her hands were still spread palms out, as if entreating him to come to her for comfort. She blinked and shook her head, trying to figure out what had just happened.

Who was Mack Griffin anyway? Was he the broken, vulnerable man who'd watched his mother get beaten to death? The way he'd been so reluctant to help her or even have anything to do with her made sense now. He was afraid he would fail to protect her like he'd failed his mom.

But this emotionless robot of a man who'd just spoken to her as if he were swatting a bothersome fly, who'd told her he cared nothing for love or tenderness and liked women who felt the same, was a totally different creature. But in a way, that made sense, too. If she believed that he'd never wanted to help her in the first place and had only done so because—

Because? *That was the problem.* Why? If he was that man, why would he have helped her at all? She didn't hesitate. She knew the answer. To get the information he needed about the man with the red tattoo. He'd done what he had to do—taken care of her, come to her rescue, had sex with her. And she'd believed it all. The tenderness, the sweetness. Because when he was close to her, she couldn't think straight.

Somehow, when he touched her, she saw the best in him. Promise, safety, temptation, even love. Was that the truth? Or was the truth that it had all been a lie? Had he just used her to find the man he believed had killed his mother?

Now that he had the information he needed about the man with the red tattoo, he had no further use for her. He'd tried to warn her, in his own way.

Hannah felt a sadness and a grief that she doubted anything would cure. She understood him now. He was both men. He was everything. Broken and unbreakable. Vulnerable and stoic. Full of revenge and full of heartache.

She turned out the lights and got into the bed, closing her burning eyes. She'd thought she would cry—for him and for herself. But she didn't. She went right to sleep.

Much later, Mack came in, stripped off his clothes and got into bed with her. He took her in his arms, the coolness of his skin giving her goose bumps at first. He kissed her and caressed her, and she did the same, until they were both hot and panting. Then he made love to her as if she was the most precious, fragile, beautiful thing he'd ever held.

After the lovemaking was over and both of them had cried out in climax then collapsed, drained and satiated, he tucked his head into the curve of her shoulder and whispered in her ear.

"I love you, Hannah. So much." His breath was hot and sweet against her ear. "As much as I can. But it's not enough. You deserve so much better than me."

THE NEXT MORNING, Mack and Hannah were in the kitchen before six o'clock, talking about the plan for the day. In front of Hannah on the kitchen table were her laptop, Billy Joe's key ring and a flat, plastic key holder that advertised an insurance company.

Hannah sipped hot coffee with sugar. "I can't even think about this," she said. "Me acting like I know about computers? I couldn't fool a four-year-old. Are you sure this is a good plan?"

"You don't have to fool anyone. You just have to be confident. You'll be sitting in front of the laptop as if you've been trying passwords all night, as if you're sure that Billy Joe hid the information about the drugs and money on his computer somewhere. I'll get the computer set up for you."

"Fine." She stood and started to pace. "Mack, my mother's appointment for dialysis was yesterday. She's going to die."

Mack caught her by her upper arms. "Listen to me," he said. "Your mom is going to be fine. You've got to believe that. And panicking doesn't help anything."

Hannah stiffened. "Let go of me," she said through clenched teeth. He did, thank goodness, because even in the middle of a panic attack, his touch rattled her. His warm fingers held too much promise, too much safety, too much temptation. And she couldn't go there. Not even if last night was real. Not even if he'd told her the truth, that he loved her. Because she knew what he'd said after that was also true. It wasn't enough.

She chafed her arms as if he'd hurt her. He hadn't—at least not physically. He'd never do that. He'd seen his mother hurt and eventually killed by men who abused women. He was the perfect protector, precisely because he had spent his life learning how not to get involved. And that broke her heart.

Mack would never admit or even believe that he needed love. He believed all he needed was revenge.

His goal was to find the man who'd killed his mother, the man with the red tattoo. Once he'd done that, he'd have no further use for her. He'd told her he didn't do relationships.

"Do you know what this is?" He showed her a tiny black plastic square.

She nodded. "I've seen them."

"It's an SD card. It stores data, like a jump drive." He inserted it into a slot in her laptop. "When the man comes in and demands to know what you know about the money, you tell him that you've been up all night trying passwords, but a little while ago you noticed something funny about the plastic key fob that held Billy Joe's keys. So you split it and discovered the SD card hidden inside. But you haven't had a chance to try it."

"That plastic holder wasn't on his key ring," she said.

"No, it wasn't, but Ficone's man won't know that. Now look. The plastic was split lengthwise and the SD was slipped right between the two layers."

Hannah examined the piece of plastic.

"Tell him you can't believe Billy Joe thought of that on his own."

"This? Oh, I can believe he thought of this. What I can't believe is that it will fool the man with the red tattoo or Ficone for more than a moment."

"A moment is all we'll need. We need to go over the rest of the plan so I can get out to the garage. I want to take a look at it in daylight. That's where the sheriff and I are going to be hiding to wait for Ficone's men. Now, Sheriff King should be here any minute, along with three of his deputies."

"Sheriff King? But he'll arrest me." Hannah's eyes went wide.

"Dawson has talked to him. We know that Hoyt, the guy in the maroon car, followed us almost all the way here before he turned south toward Galveston. Dawson's computer whiz has been tracking him using the GPS locator on his phone. What we're betting on is that he's bringing Ficone here to find the money and drugs himself."

"I don't get it. We don't know where they are. How will we convince Ficone that they're here?"

Mack folded his arms and gave her an ironic glance. "The more we act like we're searching for them here, the more Ficone will believe that we have proof of where they are."

"And the deputies are going to be in the basement?"

Mack nodded. "And you'll be right here, where we can see you and the deputies can hear you."

The kitchen table faced two large windows that looked out over the side yard, the driveway and the garage. Her mother had left them bare of curtains, and that meant that anyone who drove into the driveway or who was looking out the side door into the garage could see someone sitting at the kitchen table. "When he—or they—drive in, you'll be working on this laptop, trying passwords to get into it. You think Billy Joe stored a file in there with information about where he hid the money and the rest of the drugs."

"So all I'm doing is looking at the plastic key fob when they come in? Hopefully they won't run in firing their guns. What do you think Hoyt—or Ficone—is going to do ?"

"I *hope* he's going to take the SD card and sit down at the computer himself. That would be the best scenario. If he starts retrieving what's on the SD card, he'll be distracted and we can get the drop on him."

She looked at him. "What's the worst scenario?"

"He gets pissed off and thinks it's a setup and you're lying to him. But by then we'll be in position to get the drop on him and Sheriff King will arrest him."

"Okay," she said. "Let's do it."

Mack studied her for a moment. "You're ready?"

She shrugged. "Does it matter?"

His mouth curled. "Not a bit," he said. "Is your earpiece in place?"

She touched her ear and nodded as he checked his own.

"Go ahead and turn it on. Sheriff King has the others. We'll get them synced to the same channel when they get here."

Hannah pressed the remote control in her pocket and a faint buzzing told her the unit was on.

Mack walked to the back door and opened it. "Watch how loud you talk," he whispered, "when you're this close to the other person. You could get feedback."

She nodded again as he headed toward the garage.

She sat and inserted the SD card into the proper slot on the laptop. As she did, she wondered just how much the man with the red tattoo, or Ficone, knew about Billy Joe. Probably not as much as she did.

During the past few months while Billy Joe and her mom had dated, she had gotten the definite impression that he was hardly a great technological mind. For him, setting a reminder on his cell phone had seemed challenging. Yet Mack and his friend Dawson were banking on Ficone's people believing he had stored vital information on an SD card and password protected it.

On the laptop's screen, a window with a blank area came up with the words *enter your password.* She looked out the window toward the garage. If the card was asking for a password, did that mean that Mack or someone had put a password on it?

Mack said all they had to do was fool Ficone's man for a moment. She supposed it would help if the man saw some evidence that she'd been working on getting into the data on the card. She thought about what Billy Joe would choose as a password. Certainly nothing too complex, because it was Billy Joe. Maybe Stephanie1? Or Mustang1? Or June 11, her mother's birthday?

Then, in the distance, she heard the sound of a car engine. She froze; her breath caught in her throat as she listened. Her mouth went dry and her heart pounded. Was it the man with the red tattoo? Her rational brain said no. The sheriff was due to be here any minute. It was probably him.

She hadn't known where she was going when she'd run away from a killer five days ago. But now she did. She was headed toward this. The next minutes or hours were a matter of life or death.

MACK WENT INTO the garage by the side door. Moving all the equipment last night had probably played hell with the crime scene. He hoped the crime-scene techs were finished gathering evidence.

He looked at the place on the floor where the workbench had sat before he'd moved it. The concrete floor had been wiped down, but not cleaned thoroughly, and there were streaks of blood still there. Mack saw two places where crime-scene technicians had swabbed samples. The small streaks of their cotton swabs were clearly visible.

Mack figured the guy with the red tattoo was a professional, and if he'd had time, he'd have cleaned up Billy Joe's blood, maybe even using bleach in hopes of confusing the techs and possibly even corroding the techs' instruments.

Mack figured it wouldn't be difficult to prove that someone had bled out on the concrete floor. The hard part for Mack—or whoever Hannah hired as her lawyer—would be proving that it hadn't been Hannah.

Mack straightened. The sheriff should be here within the next ten to fifteen minutes. Meanwhile, he wanted to take a look at the workbench and see what the blood spatter looked like on it, so he walked toward the back wall of the garage.

He went over in his mind the plan that he, Sheriff King and Dawson had worked out. He was confident that they'd definitely be able to handle one or two or even three men. They should be able to handle as many as half a dozen, if they were able to get set up in place in plenty of time.

They were dealing with several unknowns. First and foremost, that Ficone's man or men would even show up this morning. That assumption was based on the man with the red tattoo telling Billy Joe that Ficone had forty-eight hours to give the money to his suppliers and the drugs to his distributors.

Mack examined the workbench. Despite some smears where he'd moved the bench the night before, the pattern of blood spatter on the workbench matched the floor and wall near the door, and matched Hannah's description of the one that had gone through Billy Joe's chest and out his back, which was why she'd seen the blood blossoming on the back of his shirt.

Now the question was, where was the bullet? Mack tried to picture exactly where the man with the red tattoo had been standing, where Billy Joe had stood, what the trajectory of the bullet had been and which way it had been traveling when it had exited Billy Joe's back. He knew that the crime-scene techs had probably measured and estimated the trajectory. He wondered if they'd found the slug. If they hadn't, maybe he could.

Chapter Fourteen

Hannah clutched at her chest as if the pressure of her hand could calm her heart. The car's engine she'd heard had not gotten louder, but had gone past and faded. It was obviously someone going by on the road. She looked out the window at the garage, wondering if Mack had heard it. She started to ask him, but they had talked about not using the earbuds for idle talk. The units were extremely powerful and therefore the batteries tended to run down very fast.

She picked up her coffee cup, dismayed when her hand trembled. She needed to calm down. It was going to be a really long, terrifying day if she jumped at every sound.

She checked the time on the laptop. It was twenty minutes to seven. Hadn't Mack said that the sheriff would be here by seven? So the next sound she heard would probably be the sheriff's truck.

She drained the last drops of coffee from her cup, wishing she'd thought to bring the coffeemaker upstairs this morning, then picked up Billy Joe's heavy key ring and dangled it from a finger, thinking how heavy it was.

Just how many keys did Billy Joe have on that ring? There had been times during these past four days when she'd have sworn that the keys added five pounds to her purse. She set her coffee cup down and counted them.

"Eighteen, nineteen," she whispered, handling the last key, which was clad with black rubber. It was the key to the Mustang. Too bad it was up on blocks. It would be a great car to drive.

She tried to remember how Billy Joe had brought it to the house and gotten it into the garage, but she couldn't. He must have brought it while she was at work or in the neighboring town of Paris for the art class she'd been taking at the community college. She'd never thought about whether he'd driven it or had it hauled. She closed her eyes and tried to remember whether it had tires or if it was literally up on blocks. If it did have tires, was it drivable?

When she opened her eyes, she was looking at the words that had come up on the computer screen when she'd inserted the SD card. *Enter your password.*

She dangled the keys, staring at the plastic key fob. Would the trick fool them? She shook the keys like cymbals, listening to their metallic clatter.

She knew Billy Joe as well as anyone. Where had he hidden the money and the drugs? She should be able to figure out his hiding place. She was a *lot* smarter than him.

And that quickly, she knew. She closed her fist around the Mustang key. She wanted to tell Mack, but not through the earbud. She wanted to show him.

They were in the Mustang! They'd been right there, behind the man with the red tattoo the whole time. That was why Billy Joe had laughed. He'd thought he was putting something over on the man, up until the instant he'd been shot.

Hannah hurried outside and headed across the driveway. The yellow crime-scene tape was ragged and torn and fluttering in the breeze like a parade of tiny yellow flags across the overhead door. Hannah saluted them as she skipped, nearly giddy with excitement that she'd solved the mystery. She couldn't wait to tell Mack.

Just as she reached for the doorknob, she heard something behind her.

MACK HEARD SOMETHING through his earbud. He stood still and listened. Had Hannah coughed or said something out loud? Then he heard it again. It was a quiet scream, this time cut off in the middle.

"Hannah, what's wrong?" he said quietly as he rushed toward the side door. But the earbud went dead. Then he saw her, through the glass panes. He stopped short.

She was in the clutches of a man who had his hand over her mouth. Mack stared at the hand. It was large and the back of the wrist was covered with a red heart tattoo with the word *MOM* in black letters inside the heart.

"Get rid of your earpiece," the man yelled. "Now!"

Mack pulled the earbud out of his ear, held it up and then tossed it on the ground. "Now open the damn door!" the man yelled. "And be careful or I'll shoot her."

Mack looked at his other hand. He was holding a gun, and the gun's barrel was sunk into Hannah's stomach. Mack opened the door.

"Back up!"

Mack backed up. He was trying to think, to improvise a plan to get the gun away from the man with the red tattoo and save Hannah, but his brain seemed frozen with shock. All he could do was obey the man's orders.

"I said back up! More!"

Mack took a couple more steps backward, doing his best to jump-start his brain. Yes, the man had a loaded gun aimed at Hannah. Yes, Mack knew that he would shoot her—but maybe not yet.

Did he still believe that she knew where the drugs and money were? Would he hold off on killing her until he'd gotten the information from her?

"Open the door," the man commanded Hannah. When she did, he sidled inside, pushing her ahead of him. Then he nudged the door closed behind him and let go of Hannah's mouth. With lightning-fast movements, he reversed the hand holding her around the waist and the hand holding the gun, then he pressed the gun up under her chin.

Watching him, Mack knew he was a professional. He knew that the best place to hold a gun for maximum impact and minimum chance for error was directly under the victim's chin, propped just inside the jawbone so she couldn't turn her head and dodge the bullet.

"Let her go," Mack said.

"Mack, I'm sorry—" Hannah started, but the man jabbed the gun more deeply into her flesh.

"Shut up!"

She nodded, her eyes on Mack, wide and wet and terrified.

Mack clenched his fists. "Damn you. There are law enforcement officers here. They probably have you in their sights right now, just waiting for the perfect shot."

"Oh, please, Mr. Griffin. Don't give me that lawyer bunk. There's nobody here. I've been looking around the area for the past hour. We're going to be done long before they arrive. I can guarantee you this is not going to take long. I just need to get rid of you and start convincing Hannah that it's in her best interest to tell me where the money and drugs are."

"She doesn't know. Nobody does. You killed the only person who could tell you."

Hannah opened her eyes wider and, without moving her head, she shifted her gaze behind him, then back at him, then behind again. Then she moved her lips.

He frowned.

The man with the red tattoo jabbed the gun into the soft flesh under her chin again, hard enough that she cried out. "What are you doing, Hannah? Why don't you tell me what you just tried to tell Mr. Griffin?"

She didn't move.

"Hannah?" He jabbed again.

"Ah!" she cried. "Nothing. It was nothing!"

The man squeezed his other arm more tightly around her waist, then turned the barrel of the gun toward Mack. "I'll kill your lawyer friend here," he said. "I promise you that."

Hannah's jaw throbbed where the gun's barrel had been pressing. It was a relief not to have the hard steel pushing into the top of her throat enough that she had trouble swallowing. But now the man was pointing the gun at Mack.

She shook her head. "No! Please, no. I'll—" Her breath caught in a sob. "I'll tell you."

"Hannah, no!" Mack cried. "You can't believe a word he says. Don't worry. I'm fine. I'll be fine. Please, Hannah, just hold on. The sheriff will be here any second."

"For what good it will do," the man said. "Come on, Hannah. Tell me."

She nodded, still looking at Mack. "Okay," she said, her chest heaving with her panicked breaths. "I told him I love him," she said. "I—just needed to say that before you—"

The man laughed. "That's so sweet, Hannah."

She felt his arm muscles tense as he lifted the barrel of the gun.

"No—please don't—" she gasped.

"Shut up," the man whispered in her ear.

Mack's face went still and he moved his gaze from her to the man holding her. He'd morphed into the emotionless robot she hated. "What's your name?" he asked the man, his voice level and detached.

Hannah felt tears fill her eyes and slip down her cheeks. "Mack, don't. Don't give him the satisfaction."

"Satisfaction?" The man's low, creepy voice sounded more animated than she'd ever heard it. Mack had intrigued him. "What in the world could give me more satisfaction than killing the two of you?"

"I asked you a question," Mack said, still no emotion in his voice.

"My name? It's Hoyt. Hoyt Diller. Why?"

"I've waited twenty years to meet you," Mack said, still no inflection in his voice. "You killed my mother."

Hannah felt Hoyt's body go tense. Mack had surprised him. He laughed. "I doubt that. In my line of work I don't get an opportunity to assassinate women very often."

"I don't think this was work," Mack said. "I think it was purely entertainment."

The man tensed even more. "Oh, yeah? What the hell are you talking about? And if all you're doing is trying to buy time, it's not going to work. I've only killed a couple of women in my life, so you've got two chances to get it right, and then—Hannah? You can say good-bye to your new boyfriend."

"No," she cried, sobbing. "No. Please don't. I'll tell you. I'll tell you everything—"

"My mother!" Mack's voice rose above hers, pulling Hoyt's attention back to him. "My mother was Kathleen Griffin, and you beat her to death right in front of me."

Hannah put her hands on top of the man's arm that was wrapped around her waist. "Please!" she sobbed. "It's in the Mustang. Everything. Billy Joe hid the money and the drugs in the Mustang. Take them to your boss. That's all you want, right? Just go and leave us alone. We'll never tell anybody—"

"Hannah!" Mack yelled, his voice no longer steady and emotionless. "Stop! My mother was your girlfriend, *Hoyt,* in Chef Voleur—"

"Oh, shut up," Hoyt spat. "Stop boring me with your pathetic story. Do you think I care about your whore of a mother? I've never been to that dumb town before. Never even heard of it."

Mack's eyes turned a peculiar color, like tarnished silver. He dived at Hoyt's feet.

"No! Mack!" she cried as a gunshot rang out. Her legs dropped right out from under her. Hoyt's arm squeezed her so tightly she couldn't catch a breath. Another loud report sounded. She screamed.

Then it seemed to her that the world exploded into volleys of gunfire. Hoyt let go of her.

The next thing she knew, she was on the ground with the smell of gun smoke in her nostrils and her eyes burning like fire. She rolled up into a ball and lay there, trying to make herself as small as possible.

"Mack?" she sobbed quietly. "Where are you? Are you okay?" Her eyes stung with smoke and tears and she couldn't hear anything except gunfire and incoherent shouts.

Mack, please be okay.

THE NEXT AFTERNOON Hannah kissed her mother on the cheek. She whispered, "'Bye, Mom. I'm sorry I have to go. I'll see you tomorrow." She didn't like her mother's color. The liver failure and dehydration had taken its toll. But the doctors assured her that the hemodialysis was doing its job and within a few days, her mom would be well enough to be discharged.

They'd also told her that because of the trauma of her abduction, her mother had been moved forward on the liver transplant list. There was a real possibility that she'd receive a liver within the next few weeks.

Her mother smiled wanly. "'Bye, sweetheart," she whispered. "Don't worry. I'm feeling better already. It's you I'm worried about. Nurse, are you sure she's ready to be discharged?"

Hannah shook her head and smiled. "There's nothing wrong with me except a cut on my forehead." But when she straightened, her head throbbed in pain and she swayed.

The nurse caught her arm. "Okay," she said. "That's enough. Sit back down in the wheelchair. I was supposed to have you downstairs five minutes ago."

Hannah sank into the chair, her head spinning. She touched her forehead where a large bandage covered what she'd been told were five stitches.

"Thanks for bringing me by to see her one more time. I don't know how long it will be before I can get back here."

"Oh, you're welcome, honey," the nurse said as she turned the wheelchair and rolled it out of the room and down the hallway of the dialysis unit to the freight elevators. "I'm taking you down the back elevators to avoid the reporters and the gawkers. There's a police car waiting for you in the basement of the parking garage."

Hannah let the nurse help her out of the wheelchair and into the backseat of the police car. During the nearly two-hour drive from the hospital to Dowdie, Hannah alternately dozed and replayed the past twenty-four hours since what she thought of as the *Shootout at the Mustang Garage*.

She had no recollection of being in an ambulance or getting the five stitches. She did remember Sheriff King visiting her in the E.R. cubicle. He'd asked her about a million questions and told her that Hoyt Diller had been taken into custody, as had Sal Ficone, who'd been picked up in the maroon sedan about a quarter mile from Hannah's house. He'd supposedly been waiting for Hoyt to take care of the dirty work. Then Ficone had planned to sweep in and take possession of the drugs and money that Billy Joe had stolen, which were found in the Mustang, under the seats, exactly where Hannah had said they had to be.

The sheriff had also told her that her mother was upstairs in the hemodialysis unit and was apparently doing fine.

He hadn't offered anything about Mack, though, so Hannah had asked.

"He's okay. Took a bullet in his left arm, but that's it. He was discharged. I'm not sure where he is tonight, but tomorrow he'll be at my office, just like you, answering questions and filling out forms."

She'd been discharged from the E.R. and had spent the rest of the day and overnight in her mom's room.

She'd hardly slept at all. She'd spent most of the time talking to her mom or holding her hand while she slept.

Hannah was dozing in the car when the change in engine sound told her the police car was slowing to a stop. The officer driving got out and came around to help her out of the backseat and into the Dowdie Sheriff's office.

Sheriff King met them at the door and guided her back to a room with a big wooden table, a refrigerator, a microwave and a coffeepot full of what smelled like fresh coffee.

"Want a cup?" the sheriff asked her.

"Please," Hannah said. "With lots of sugar."

He poured the coffee and set the cup, a spoon and a box of sugar cubes in front of her. She dropped seven cubes into the cup and stirred it, watching the dark bubbles rise and burst on the coffee's surface. She was just taking her first swallow when the door to the room opened.

She looked up and nearly choked on the coffee. It was Mack. He had on blue scrubs and his left arm was bandaged and in a sling. She breathed deeply. The sheriff had told her he was all right, but it was a huge relief to see him for herself. The last time she'd seen him he'd been diving at Hoyt.

He took in the room with a quick glance, nodded briefly at her then walked over to the coffeepot and clumsily poured himself a cup. He sat down opposite her.

She lowered her gaze to her coffee again, but she could feel his eyes on her. She looked up, clearing her throat quietly. "Hi," she said.

He took a swallow of coffee. "Hi," he muttered.

"You're okay?"

He nodded. "You?"

"I'm fine." She touched the bandage on her forehead with a sheepish smile. "Five stitches. Hardly the badge of courage you have there. What happened to you?"

He grimaced and gave a little shake of his head. "Took a bullet. Went straight through the biceps without hitting anything. It's fine." He paused. "I heard your mom's going to be okay."

His casual mention of her mother made her angry. Her scalp tightened and a place in her chest burned. "She's going to be fine. Why didn't you tell me you'd found her? I had to find out from Sheriff King that she was safe on the hemodialysis ward. The nurses told me she'd been there for almost twenty-four hours."

Mack's jaw tensed. "Your life was in danger. I couldn't risk you running off to the hospital in the middle of everything because you had to see your mother."

"What did you think would happen?" she asked sarcastically. "The bad guy would grab me?"

Mack sent her a disgusted look.

Part of why she was so angry with him was because she knew he was right. She definitely would have wanted to rush to her mother. Would she have? She couldn't say. "Where was she? And how did you find her?"

"Dawson had Dusty, his computer person, looking all over the area for an apartment rented to Billy Joe Campbell. Dawson's wife called all the hospitals. When neighbors complained about loud music coming from an apartment in Paris, the police found her. She'd been locked in the bathroom."

Hannah nodded, her eyes stinging.

"Thank you for saving her," Hannah said politely, although inside, she felt as though she was about to explode. How long were they going to sit here like two people discussing last night's game around the water cooler? She was sick of his calm exterior, his even tone, his carefully studied disinterest. She had to do something to provoke a response in him—positive or negative, it hardly mattered.

"So, Mack, did you get what you wanted from the man with the red tattoo?" She tried to emulate him. Tried to keep her voice as steady as she could.

She saw his jaw muscle tense and flex. She waited, holding her breath, but he didn't answer. He drank his coffee without looking at her.

"Well?" she prompted. "Was him calling your mother a whore what you were going for?"

Mack set his coffee cup down carefully. "Hannah," he said warningly. "Don't—"

"Don't what? I want to know, Mack. I'm curious. You found him—the man who killed your mother. Did it help?"

He shook his head, then looked up at her, and what she saw broke her heart. His green-gold eyes were dark and bottomless with pain. "It wasn't him." He grasped the cup at the rim and twirled it on the table, watching it spin around and around.

This time when he looked at her, his mouth was twisted into an ironic smile. "Ficone has the same tattoo. Apparently, the patriarch, Marco, I think was his name, designed the tattoo as a tribute to his mother, and had all his hit men get it so rival families would know who they were dealing with. His boy, Sal, has continued the tradition. There may be a dozen guys who have the same tattoo."

"Oh, no," Hannah said. "I'm so sorry. You must be devastated."

He stood and turned away to put his cup in the sink. "I've got to go. I just wanted—" he cleared his throat "—a cup of coffee before my turn to be grilled by the sheriff."

Hannah stood, too, and watched him as he turned toward the door. She waited, hoping against hope that he would turn around. But he didn't. Just at the moment when he was about to step across the threshold of the door, she spoke. "Mack?"

He stopped, but didn't turn around.

"Mack, turn around and look at me, please."

Nothing.

She swallowed and her throat tried to contract. "I love you," she said softly. For a long time, nothing happened.

Then Mack lowered his head and rubbed the back of his neck.

"I love you," she said again.

He made a sound, deep in his throat. It was a groan or a moan.

"I love you." To her chagrin, her eyes began to sting. "I love—"

Mack turned. "Hannah, don't do this, please. I've tried to explain—"

"I love you, Mack," she said. "And I know you love me. *I know it.* You have to trust me. And you have to trust yourself. I don't know why you don't. You were born to be a protector. You saved me."

She saw his throat move as he swallowed and shook his head. "I nearly got you killed."

"If you hadn't helped me, I'd have died," she said. "You saved me."

He shook his head. "It's not—"

"I love you," she interrupted. "And you love me."

This time, to her surprise, he nodded. "I do. I love you. But it's not enough."

She smiled at him. "It will always be enough."

Mack took a step toward her.

She lifted her head and smiled at him.

He took a second step and wrapped his good arm around her and pulled her close. He buried his nose in her hair and held her, so tightly that she found it hard to breathe. He kissed her hair gently, then the bandage at her forehead, then the tip of her nose and her mouth. His kiss was soft at first, but when she opened to him, he kissed her more deeply and intimately, until both of them were panting with desire.

Hannah heard footsteps, which paused in the doorway. Sheriff King cleared his throat. "I'll come back later," he mumbled.

She chuckled, breaking the spell of the kiss. Mack pulled back, a smile on his face and a glimmer of wonder in his eyes. "I guess we've got to take care of this business before we can deal with *us*."

She nodded. "Should we go find the sheriff and tell him he can come back now?"

Mack nodded, his smile fading. "Hannah," he said, "This isn't going to be easy."

"I don't think either one of us expects easy."

"I'm kind of a mess," he went on. "I've got a lot of issues."

Hannah kissed him lightly on the cheek. "Then we make quite a pair, don't we?"

Epilogue

Two weeks from the day they caught Sal Ficone, Mack smiled at Hannah as she hung up from talking to her mom.

"How is she?" he asked. "Just fine. Right?"

Hannah nodded reluctantly. "Yes, she's fine. Yes, she's in the hospital. Yes, she's safe. But I'm still not sure…"

"Shh," Mack said, pulling her close in the confines of the taxi that was speeding through the streets of Paris. "You're doing exactly the right thing. Your mom would be all over you if you'd refused to take this trip."

She sighed. "I feel so torn. I know Mom's okay right now, but how much longer can she wait for a new liver? My grandmother sounded well, but it's only been a few days since her heart attack."

Mack looked out the taxi window. "Which is why we're going to her house, rather than having her take a taxi to the hotel. You'd never forgive yourself if you hadn't come and something happened to Claire."

"That's what's tearing me apart. I could lose either of them in a heartbeat." She touched Mack's arm. "And what if a liver becomes available, like, tonight?"

"You know what the doctor said. That's why she's right there in the hospital. And we can be in Dallas within several hours."

"And we'll be there four days from now, on Monday anyway, for Sal Ficone's arraignment," Mack reminded her as the taxi spun in a U-turn and pulled to the curb in front of a lovely old house.

"Oh. Is this Rue de Jonge?" Hannah put her phone in her purse. She got out while Mack paid the driver. Then the two of them walked up to the door.

"Oh, Mack," she said, practically speechless with emotion. "This is so unbelievable. I have—no, *we* have a new family, and I hardly know any of them."

Mack kissed her forehead, where a small bandage had taken the place of the large one. "I've already told you, the Delanceys are quite a crowd."

"And now we're meeting the grandmother I never knew." She patted her hair then turned to look at him. "Where's your sling? You're not supposed to take it off."

Mack's eyes sparkled. "Probably in the bed back in the hotel room."

"You can't just ignore what the doctors said. You're supposed to wear it all the time…. It's going to be quite a while before we're able to settle down in Chef Voleur," Hannah said.

"Don't worry about that. I'm fine as long as I'm with you," Mack murmured in her ear as the front door opened and a petite woman with a gray braid wrapped elegantly around the crown of her head, and wearing a gorgeous couture pantsuit and four-inch Jimmy Choo shoes, stood there, beaming. "Hannah? And Mack?" she said. Hannah just stood there smiling, seemingly unable to speak.

"Hannah, I'm your grandmother," the tiny woman said. "You're welcome to call me Grandmother, Grandmere or Claire." Claire took a step back and gestured for them to enter. The living room appeared to take up the entire first floor. It was sparsely furnished and a hand-painted mandala was the focal point on the expanse of hardwood on the floor.

Hannah felt Mack's hand on the small of her back, warm and reassuring. She stepped inside, with him at her side.

Then she held out her arms. "I want to call you Grandmother," she said, wrapping her arms around the smaller woman. Her grandmother had a strong, vital presence, but in Hannah's embrace, she felt tiny and frail. Hannah's heart twisted.

Then Claire pushed her away to look at her. "Oh, my goodness, you look just like your grandfather."

"M-my grandfather?"

"Ektor," Claire said. "Ektor Petrakis. Stephanie was the spitting image of him when she was a baby." A shadow crossed Claire's face. "How is your mother?"

"She's actually doing okay. She's in the hospital, due to receive a liver transplant any day now."

"Oh, I'm so glad." Claire stared into space for a few seconds, then turned her attention back to Hannah.

"My dear, you are so beautiful." Claire took Hannah's hand in hers, then she reached out her other hand for Mack's. Hannah glanced at him and found him grinning as if she was his newfound grandmother. "Come in. Come in. We have café au lait or tea, and I have madeleines from the bakery on the corner. Sit and let's talk."

She pulled them to one corner of the large room where two sofas faced each other in a small conversation area near a window.

"I want to hear everything, Hannah, from the moment you were born." She laughed, and the sound of her laughter was like a chorus of small bells. "I need enough information to hold me until I can get my doctor to let me fly to Texas to visit my daughter, and have another, hopefully longer, visit with you."

"As soon as Mom can travel after her liver transplant, we're going to take her to live in Chef Voleur with us. We've decided that the hometown of the Delanceys will be our home, and I want my mom and you, if you'll agree, with us," Hannah said. "And so does Mack."

Hannah glanced at Mack, who had not sat, but was walking around looking at the art pieces placed strategically around the room. He smiled at her, then at her grandmother. "We'd be honored, Ms. Delancey."

"Oh, child," Claire said. "Call me Claire or Grandmother."

Mack sent Hannah a quick look, then grinned at Claire. "Ma'am, it would be my great honor to call you Grandmother."

Hannah felt tears sting her eyes. Something felt odd in her chest, too. She pressed her hand there, right below her collarbone, and realized that the empty, lonely spot under her breastbone no longer felt empty. It felt full, with love and happiness. With her grandmother and her mother. With Mack.

And the desolate, uncertain future she'd seen before her just a few days before now stretched like the beautiful, mighty Mississippi River, drawing her to the town of Chef Voleur, where her family was. Where she would always be safe and loved.

* * * * *

THE DELANCEY DYNASTY *comes to an end*
with BLOOD TIES IN CHEF VOLEUR,
on sale next month
wherever Harlequin Intrigue books are sold!

COMING NEXT MONTH FROM

H HARLEQUIN®

I N T R I G U E®

Available July 15, 2014

#1509 KCPD PROTECTOR
The Precinct • by Julie Miller

A mysterious stalker threatens Elise Brown, executive assistant to KCPD's deputy commissioner, George Madigan. As George's role goes from protector to lover, will he become the one who can finally bring this brave woman her happily-ever-after?

#1510 EVIDENCE OF PASSION
Shadow Agents: Guts and Glory • by Cynthia Eden

Rachel Mancini trusted the wrong man—and nearly lost her life. Now she's in the sights of a killer, and in order to survive she has to put all of her faith in ex-SEAL Dylan Foxx. Dylan won't let her go, even if he has to break the law in order to keep her safe.

#1511 BRIDEGROOM BODYGUARD
Shotgun Weddings • by Lisa Childs

The only way for Sharon Wells to protect the child in her care is to marry the baby's father, bodyguard Parker Payne, a man she barely knows. Can Parker corner the vengeful killer who has put a hit on his new family?

#1512 SECRET OBSESSION • by Robin Perini

Desperate to keep a precious secret, Lyssa Cafferty must count on her murdered fiancé's best friend—ex-marine Noah Bradford—to save her from a killer's vicious obsession.

#1513 HUNTED
The Men from Crow Hollow • by Beverly Long

Chandler McCann needs former army helicopter pilot Ethan Moore's help to prove that her stepmother committed treason. But Ethan has enemies of his own who won't stop until Ethan loses everything—including Chandler. Can Ethan capture a traitor and Chandler's heart?

#1514 BLOOD TIES IN CHEF VOLEUR
The Delancey Dynasty • by Mallory Kane

What better way for Jacques Broussard to get vengeance on the Delancey family than seducing Cara Lynn Delancey and breaking her heart?
But when an enemy is roused and all sorts of family secrets come spilling out, will Jack's heart be the one left broken?

**YOU CAN FIND MORE INFORMATION ON UPCOMING HARLEQUIN® TITLES,
FREE EXCERPTS AND MORE AT WWW.HARLEQUIN.COM.**

HICNM0714

REQUEST YOUR FREE BOOKS!
2 FREE NOVELS PLUS 2 FREE GIFTS!

♦HARLEQUIN®

INTRIGUE®

BREATHTAKING ROMANTIC SUSPENSE

YES! Please send me 2 FREE Harlequin Intrigue® novels and my 2 FREE gifts (gifts are worth about $10). After receiving them, if I don't wish to receive any more books, I can return the shipping statement marked "cancel." If I don't cancel, I will receive 6 brand-new novels every month and be billed just $4.74 per book in the U.S. or $5.24 per book in Canada. That's a savings of at least 14% off the cover price! It's quite a bargain! Shipping and handling is just 50¢ per book in the U.S. and 75¢ per book in Canada.* I understand that accepting the 2 free books and gifts places me under no obligation to buy anything. I can always return a shipment and cancel at any time. Even if I never buy another book, the two free books and gifts are mine to keep forever.

182/382 HDN F42N

Name	(PLEASE PRINT)
Address	Apt. #
City	State/Prov.	Zip/Postal Code

Signature (if under 18, a parent or guardian must sign)

Mail to the **Harlequin® Reader Service:**
IN U.S.A.: P.O. Box 1867, Buffalo, NY 14240-1867
IN CANADA: P.O. Box 609, Fort Erie, Ontario L2A 5X3
**Are you a subscriber to Harlequin Intrigue books
and want to receive the larger-print edition?
Call 1-800-873-8635 or visit www.ReaderService.com.**

* Terms and prices subject to change without notice. Prices do not include applicable taxes. Sales tax applicable in N.Y. Canadian residents will be charged applicable taxes. Offer not valid in Quebec. This offer is limited to one order per household. Not valid for current subscribers to Harlequin Intrigue books. All orders subject to credit approval. Credit or debit balances in a customer's account(s) may be offset by any other outstanding balance owed by or to the customer. Please allow 4 to 6 weeks for delivery. Offer available while quantities last.

Your Privacy—The Harlequin® Reader Service is committed to protecting your privacy. Our Privacy Policy is available online at www.ReaderService.com or upon request from the Harlequin Reader Service.

We make a portion of our mailing list available to reputable third parties that offer products we believe may interest you. If you prefer that we not exchange your name with third parties, or if you wish to clarify or modify your communication preferences, please visit us at www.ReaderService.com/consumerschoice or write to us at Harlequin Reader Service Preference Service, P.O. Box 9062, Buffalo, NY 14269. Include your complete name and address.

HI13R

SPECIAL EXCERPT FROM

I N T R I G U E

*Rachel Mancini trusted the wrong man—and nearly lost her life.
Now she's in the sights of a killer, and in order to survive she has to
put all of her faith in former SEAL Dylan Foxx. He's been the sexy
ex-lawyer's friend for years and will do anything to keep her safe.
And though it could prove fatal,
he wants her in his arms....*

Read on for a sneak peek of
EVIDENCE OF PASSION
by New York Times *bestselling author*

Cynthia Eden

"Dylan?" Her voice was so soft that she wasn't even sure he'd heard her.

He didn't respond, but he did lead her through the crowd, pulling her toward the door. Bodies brushed against her, making Rachel tense, then they were outside. The night air was crisp, and taxis rushed by them on the busy street.

Dylan still held her hand.

He turned and pulled her toward the side of the brick building. Then he caged her with his body. "Want to tell me what you were doing?" An edge of anger had entered his words.

Rachel blinked at him. "Uh, getting a drink?" That part had seemed pretty obvious.

"What you were doing with the blond, Rachel? The blond jerk who was leaning way too close to you in that pub."

The same way that Dylan had been leaning close?

"Now isn't the time for you to start looking for a new guy." *Definite* anger now. "We need to find out if Jack is back here, killing. We don't need you to hook up with some—"

She shoved against his chest.

The move caught them both off guard.

Beneath the streetlamp, Rachel saw Dylan's eyes widen.

"You don't get to control my personal life," Rachel told him flatly. *What personal life?* The fact that she didn't have one wasn't the point. "And neither does Jack. Got it?"

He gazed back at her.

"On missions, I follow your orders. But what I do on my own time… that's *my* business." She stalked away from him, heading back toward her apartment building.

Then she heard the distinct thud of his footsteps as Dylan rushed after her. *He'd better be coming to apologize.*

Right. She'd never actually heard Dylan apologize for anything.

His fingers curled around her arm. He spun her back to face him. "Your last lover was a killer. I'd think that you'd want to—"

"You're wrong!" The words erupted from her.

And something strange happened to Dylan's face. They were right under the streetlight, so it was incredibly easy for her to read his expression. Surprise flashed first, slackening his mouth, but then fury swept over his face. A hard mask of what truly looked like rage. *"You're involved with someone else? You're sleeping with someone?"*

Since when did she have to check in with Dylan about her love life? "He wasn't my lover."

His hold tightened on her. "What?"

"Adam. Jack. Whatever he's calling himself. He. Wasn't. My. Lover." There. She'd said it. It felt good to get that out. "We were going away together that weekend. We hadn't…" Rachel cleared her throat. "He wasn't my lover." She yanked away from him, angry now, too. "Not that it's any of your business who I'm sleeping with—"

"It is." He snarled the words as he yanked her up against his chest. "It shouldn't be…but it is."

And his mouth took hers.

Dylan won't let Rachel go, even if he has to
break the law in order to keep her safe….

Don't miss the next installment in **Shadow Agents: Guts and Glory,**
EVIDENCE OF PASSION
by New York Times *bestselling author Cynthia Eden.*
On sale August 2014, only from Harlequin Intrigue.

HIEXP69777

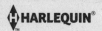

INTRIGUE

USA TODAY BESTSELLING AUTHOR
JULIE MILLER
RETURNS TO *THE PRECINCT* WITH A TALE OF A KILLER ON THE LOOSE AND A TORNADO ABOUT TO HIT KANSAS CITY

There is no way Deputy Commissioner George Madigan is going to let his beautiful assistant fall prey to a stalker. Because Elise Brown isn't just another employee. Her vulnerable blue eyes trigger all of George's protective instincts…and now her life is in jeopardy.

Working together almost 24/7 to bring the perp to justice—and sharing kisses passionate enough to ignite a Kansas City heat wave—George and Elise forge the kind of partnership that could keep her out of harm's way and potentially lead to happily-ever-after.

Until a deadly tornado strikes and Elise is taken hostage…

KCPD PROTECTOR
BY JULIE MILLER

Only from Harlequin® Intrigue®. Available August 2014 wherever books and ebooks are sold.